I0690609

THE BLACKSMITH AND THE SCHOLAR

First Edition

Published by The Nazca Plains Corporation
Las Vegas, Nevada
2011

ISBN: 978-1-61098-031-9
E-book: 978-1-61098-032-6

Published by

The Nazca Plains Corporation ®
4640 Paradise Rd, Suite 141
Las Vegas NV 89109-8000

PUBLISHER'S NOTE
The Blacksmith and the Scholar is a work of fiction created wholly
by *Bob Archman*'s imagination. All characters are fictional and any
resemblance to any persons living or deceased is purely by accident.
No portion of this book reflects any real person or events.

Male Cover Photo, Olly
Art Director, Blake Stephens

THE BLACKSMITH AND THE SCHOLAR

First Edition

Bob Archman

CONTENTS

CONTENTS CONTINUED...

CHAPTER 1

I had an idyllic childhood. When one reads the novels of Dickens, it might appear that childhoods in England were nightmares. My mother was a loving and beautiful woman. I was the only child and she devoted her life to me. My father was an inventor and industrialist. He devoted most of his life to work and when I was younger, he was aloof and distant with me.

However, when I got older he was helpful with my studies. Looking back, I don't think he knew how to deal with a small child. Queen Victoria knighted my father in 1874, becoming Sir Angus Fairbairn. This was the great event of my youth. While I was too young to attend the ceremony, all discussed it. At that time, we moved from a house in York to country house outside the city. My parents hired tutors and I did well in my studies. My life was somewhat solitary but I liked my tutors and loved my parents. I didn't miss playing with other children.

My mother was beautiful, but not strong. I when I was sixteen, I noticed my mother was becoming weaker and she had a bad cough. She died on my seventeenth birthday. This was a disaster in my life, but it occurred as I was preparing to go to Oxford and soon the excitement of leaving home for the University dulled the pain.

Oxford was a revelation to me. My life at home was conventional in the extreme. Oxford was filled with exciting men and ideas. I fell under the influence of men like William Morris and John Ruskin. Art and the Aesthetes enthralled me. Art and beauty had played no role in my life to that point. For the first time I saw Greek and Roman sculptures and Renaissance paintings. This was a new world to me, but my best friends at Oxford, Tristan Butler and Ovid Mills, were very confident, and I fell totally under their spell.

As Robert Fairbairn, son and heir of Sir Angus Fairbairn, I had a privileged life. By the standards of Oxford, I came from a modest, if not humble, background. It seemed Tristan and Ovid' s intellectual purity elevated me to the level of the sons of dukes and lords who made up a good proportion of the students.

Their taste for art was associated with purity and chastity. Purity was the watchword. This suited me, for I was both ignorant and frightened of my sexual urges. I suspected the worst of my own inclinations. Chastity was a way to avoid the issue. My friends were so self-assured; I knew they had no concerns like mine. At the end of my second term at Oxford, I went with Tristan to visit his home in southern Scotland. We took the train to York, and then undertook a memorably uncomfortable carriage ride to his distant home. We were almost halfway to his home when the carriage broke an axle and the carriage tipped over on its side.

I was unhurt, but Tristan seriously injured his leg and the driver was even more badly hurt. We were in a very secluded part of Yorkshire and the only inhabitant nearby was a blacksmith. That man had a massive dray horse, pulled the carriage off the men, and got blankets for them. He sent his boy apprentice to get help. The boy returned with a small carriage. There was no doctor nearby. It was big enough to carry the injured men and a driver. It wasn't big enough to hold me. I would walk beside the carriage. I helped get Tristan into the carriage, but hurt my back lifting Tristan.

I had never felt pain like this, but the smith knew what had happened. He said I had thrown my back out. He thought travel was out of the question for me. We decided I would stay with Ralph until I could travel. I didn't want to do this, but there didn't seem to be an alternative. I put a brave face on it. Tristan and injured driver left me alone with the hulking blacksmith.

"What's your name?" he asked. "I'm Ralph Robertson." I gave him my name and he took me to his cottage.

While Ralph was a giant of a man, he was soft spoken and polite, I had never been with a man quite like him. His cottage was modest but clean. It was entirely without refinements or luxuries. He lived alone with a large dog, named Gulliver. The boy who went to get help lived at home with his family, so he lived alone. I sat in a big, wooden chair, crudely made, but surprisingly comfortable for a man in my situation.

Luckily, Ralph knew much about back problems. I assumed they were typical for a heavy laborer like a blacksmith. He wrapped me in a warm blanket and sat me in a sunny window while he went about his work.

At the end of his workday, he went to the side of the house, stripped off his soot-covered clothes and washed himself. I had never seen a grown man naked before. I was both shocked and excited in a way I had never been before. I had seen statues of nude Greek gods and goddesses in museums, but they were nothing like Ralph, with the possible exception of the Greek hero Hercules. Ralph had the body of Hercules, but a thick coat of curly, blondish-red hair covered him.

There was another difference. The genitals of the classical statues had either delicate, elegant boy like members, or were covered with modest fig leaves. There was nothing modest or boy like about

Ralph's member. His foreskin covered a tube of flesh with a bulge the size of a small apple indicating the location of his knob. His sack seemed to hold a pair of good- sized potatoes.

My friend Ovid described the Greek sculptures as the ultimate in refinement, and expressing man's triumph over our animalistic tendencies. It seemed to me Ralph still had many of his animalistic characteristics still intact. As I watched him wash in the side yard of his cottage, I realized I had some of those tendencies too. I felt desire.

I myself didn't look much like a Greek god. I am a little above average height and weight and at age 20, hair covered my chest, and a path of hair connected my chest hair with my bush. As I watched Ralph, my cock got hard.

Ralph dried himself in the sun, dressed in clean clothes and returned to the cottage. He asked me how I felt. I said the chair was comfortable. When I tried to get up, a spasm of pain swept over me. He told me to stay still and he would make dinner. As the sun set, the cottage got cold, but the fire soon warmed the place.

The dog never let Ralph get out of his sight, but he sat next to me. I guessed I was in Ralph's chair and Gulliver was in his normal place. Ralph helped me get up and I got over to a small table where we ate simple dinner. Afterward he asked if I liked to play checkers. I did. He cleared off the mismatched plates and brought out a checkerboard. It was hand made of inlayed wood and was quite beautifully crafted. I commented on that.

"My father made it," Ralph said. "He was a cabinet maker. My older brother continued in that trade, but I wasn't good at it. I apprenticed to Old Henry, the local blacksmith, and here I am."

"It's a hard and dirty trade," I said.

"It suits me well," Ralph replied. "I like hard work." We played the game. Much to my surprise Ralph beat me. I must have looked disappointed when he won. He noticed.

"I must have gotten lucky," he said. He had noticed my disappointment. "You'll win the next time."

I felt ashamed of myself. In the intellectual circles, I moved in Oxford there was a lot of talk about the value of labor and the plight of the worker. In spite of all the talk, I was a gentleman. Ralph was a laborer. It didn't seem right that he would beat me. I tried to make amends.

"I'm afraid your good luck is due to your skills at playing the game," I said. "You won fair and square, and if I manage to win it will be due to my skills, and a little good luck." Ralph smiled. He understood what I was saying. I did manage to win a game, but that was because he made a mistake.

"I have only one bed," he said. "You can have it and I will take the chair." The bed was large.

"I don't want to force you out of the bed. We can share it, if you don't mind," I said.

"It's warmer that way," Ralph said. We went to his bed and he took off his clothes. Much to my surprise, he stripped naked. Then he helped me strip. It didn't seem to occur to him that I didn't sleep naked. I thought about objecting, but didn't. By the time I was naked my cock was excited.

"You have a nice one," he said when he saw me partly erect. Ralph helped ease me into the bed. Any wrong move was painful. Pulling blankets over me, he got in the other side of the bed.

"I haven't shared a bed since Old Henry and I slept together," Ralph said. "It was the only way to stay warm in this cold house."

"You liked your master?" I asked.

"He was a good man, quiet but friendly," Ralph said. "My father was good too, but he was a strict Presbyterian. Old Henry liked some fun. He was a bachelor, so I was the son he never had."

I had never been in bed with a naked men and the situation continued to excite me. Ralph was huge and his hairy body touched mine. The covers were cold and a bit damp. I shivered and he put his arm around me.

"Don't worry sir. I'll keep you warm," he whispered. "Cold is bad for your back." His body was warm. I was afraid he would discover I was erect. I didn't need to worry. Ralph reached for my cock and stroked it.

"It's nice and long," he said. "I didn't guess you were so big. You're a manly man. It's hard to tell under a gentleman's clothes." I was shocked. I had no idea what to do. I thought I should run from the bed, but my back made that difficult. After a minute or two, the pleasure made it impossible.

"That feels good," I said. I lied. It was more than good. I had played with myself and always felt guilty. Some of my friends talked about sexual pleasure. The pleasure I felt when I played with myself didn't seem to justify the guilt. As Ralph's meaty hand stroked my cock, it was a level of pleasure I had not felt before. Indeed, I didn't even know it existed.

Ralph seemed to know this. "This is new to you?" He asked.

"Completely," I replied. "It's wonderful."

"It's the best feeling in the world," he said. "Nothing compares to it." He chuckled. "If you're a good sport, it can get a lot better. Are you an adventurous mood?"

"I'm afraid I'm more of a scholar than an adventurer," I said. "Can you tell me what you're thinking about?"

"Man play is easier to do than to explain," Ralph explained. He stroked my cock a few times and I shivered. "One part of you knows what feels good. Just relax and let old Ralph show you the ropes."

"I don't know."

"You are more of a man of action than you think," he said. He slowly moved so we were facing each other in the bed. He slipped under the bedclothes and a second or two later he swallowed my cock. The sensations were heavenly.

After a minute or so of this, his head appeared next to me. "That was wonderful," I said.

'You were really close to shooting the cream," he said. "I was going to have little more fun before I milk you."

"Milk me?" I asked. I didn't know exactly what that was. I did have a good guess, but I couldn't believe he would do that.

Ralph laughed. "Old Henry always said a shot of warm milk before you go to bed makes you sleepy," he said. "Draining the balls every day is good for you too, I think."

"I heard it leads to weakness," I said.

Ralph laughed again. "If it does it never had any effect on Henry or me! I never miss a day and Henry could shoot off two or three times even when he got older."

"He sounds like a right randy old gentleman," I said.

"That might be true," Ralph admitted, "but I know for a fact he didn't have a mean bone in his body. He was the best master a boy could wish."

"He didn't take advantage of you?"

"Shit no," Ralph exclaimed. "I was a solid six foot tall when I was 14. I was no refined lady being used by an unfeeling cad. Henry always gave more than he took. If you gave him a shilling, he would pay you back with a pound. He was a great bedmate for a cold cottage."

"I'm warm now," I said. He was all but lying on me. His body heat was all I needed to keep warm. He shifted and I could play with his privates. They looked impressive when he washed in the yard earlier. Now they were huge. His balls were actually heavy. I stroked his pole and a wave of desire swept over me.

"Henry liked his milk warm and straight from the spigot. It was best when you let it simmer then worked it up to a boil," Ralph said. "It was a sure way to insure a good night's sleep."

Ralph didn't ask me what I wanted. He knew. He moved and fed me his cock. For a second or two I hesitated. I licked his knob. I don't know what I expected, but I loved it. I tried to get his huge knob onto my mouth. I didn't succeed, but my tongue discovered his piss slit.

Actually, I found a sweet thick liquid and followed it to the source, his slit. I loved it and soon tried to get my tongue into it. His slit was wide and I tried to get deep into the opening. As I did, I coaxed more of the fluid from his body. I was mad with desire.

Somehow, Ralph almost floated above me. He sucked my cock and I sucked his. Since we were connected only by our cocks, there was no stress on my back. He swallowed my entire cock. That was too much for me. I shot my load into his mouth. A second later, my mouth filled with Ralph's man seed. The seed wasn't as tasty as the stuff that drooled from his cock before, but I took it all. Ralph carefully shifted his position and we fell asleep.

When I woke the next morning, my back was a little better. Sunlight filled the room, and Ralph was still in bed with me. As I moved, he woke.

He got up and I had a chance to see his naked body close up. He stood next to me. His cock was at eye level. "Have you ever taken a long look at man's tool?" Ralph asked. I will swear he was a mind reader. "Take your time. It's Sunday, my day of rest," he said. His cock was soft and thick foreskin covered his knob. He peeled it back to expose the head. A bead of fluid peaked from the slit. I involuntarily stuck out my tongue.

Ralph smiled. "I see you like the ball juice."

"What is it?"

"I don't know what the real name is. Henry called it love juice or cock jelly," Ralph said. "It comes before the main load."

"That's the bitter, salty stuff?"

"That's it. You get to like it after a while. Yours is good, rich and creamy. Did you like mine?"

"I don't know," I said. Ralph looked disappointed. "I may need to try it a few more times."

He smiled. "Maybe we can work on that today."

I moved so I could get his cock again. I twisted the wrong way and winced. Ralph moved and I sucked him. When I started, he was soft and his member grew as I ministered to it. I was inordinately pleased. I was able to give him pleasure. It was such a simple thing. I sucked him and he responded.

"I am a novice in these matters," I said after our second coupling. "I truthfully didn't know these things were possible. It is a new world of sensation. How did you discover all of this?"

"Old Henry knew a lot, but mostly we learned by trial and error," Ralph answered.

"The trial part I understand," I observed. "The error part might not be that good."

"As I told you, Old Henry was a good man. Winter nights are long and cold. We had all the time in the world to explore," Ralph explained. "We had the time and the inclination. We had fun too. Henry was full of curiosity and enthusiasm. He also liked to teach others his skills."

"Were you his only student?" I asked.

"Not hardly," Ralph replied. "You could say he ran an academy of the sexual arts. There's no need to keep your knowledge to yourself," he'd say. "Spread the wealth." He had a knack for finding like minded bachelors."

"You got a degree from his academy?" I asked.

Ralph laughed. "That I did, but truthfully speaking, it was hard to fail at his course of studies. Old Henry was a good teacher and you could say the subject matter all but taught itself." He looked me in the eye. "I'd like to teach you what he taught me," he said.

"I don't know if I could do that," I replied.

"Let me assure you that you would have no problem becoming a star student at all," he said. "You're a smart lad, but I'm afraid you do too much thinking with your brain, and not enough with your cock." He felt for my cock. I was hard. "Was last night the first time you were in bed with a bare-naked man?" He asked.

I nodded.

"Let yourself go. Jump into it with both feet." he said. "You can't be half a virgin. Once you've made your first step into the art of man love, you might as well go all the way." He groped my genitals again. I was going to protest that I wasn't that interested, but my erect genitals would undermine my sincerity. I looked him in the eyes and he smiled. He knew I was willing.

"I have a confession to make," Ralph said. "Several old friends are coming over today. "

"Are they graduates of Old Henry's academy?" I asked.

He smiled. "They are. Don't worry, they are good men and good sports too," Ralph said. "You will like them."

As we talked, the sunny sky of the morning had vanished and the house was now dark. A clap of thunder announced a storm. Ralph's cottage was an old stone dwelling that was damp and cold by its nature. While it was early summer, the storm was more of a winter gale. As the wind blew any trace of warmth in the dwelling vanished. Ralph added a log to the fire.

He helped me get dressed and made a simple breakfast. Everything was simple and plain, but satisfying and comfortable. I knew I should have been uncomfortable with the huge man, but I instinctively knew he was a good man. If he said his friends were good sports, I believed him. One part of me was afraid of meeting Ralph's playmates, but the far greater part was excited at the prospect. The night before, Ralph opened the door to a world of pleasure and excitement I hadn't known existed. I was going to go through the door.

At mid-day, someone rapped at the door. Ralph opened it and six men entered, covered in soaking wet clothes. They looked like drowned sheepdogs. One was a child. That I hadn't expected. Ralph greeted them heartily and added more wood to the fire. The men stripped off their sodden clothes and hung them by the fire to dry.

They were all naked and huddled by the fire when they noticed me. "Who is the new lad, Ralph?" a big bear like man asked. Even though he was naked in front of a man he had never seen before, he seemed curious and not at all embarrassed.

"Men this is Robert Fairbairn, a scholar from Oxford. He injured himself trying to help his traveling companions when their coach broke down. He hurt his back and is here until he can travel," Ralph explained. "He's a bachelor like us. He isn't a man of broad experience, but he is a fast learner."

"Welcome to our merry band," the child said in a deep bass voice. I did a double take. The child was a full-grown man who was half sized. "I am Robert too," he said as he shook my hand.

"Welcome," the bear like man said, "I'm Angus, and this is my son, Alexander." Angus was as muscular as Ralph was, but not as tall and was covered in curly black hair. Alexander was a taller, but thinner version of his father. "We're stone masons. Robert works for us, but he's a carver. Very skilled he is."

"I'm William the miller," a smaller man said.

"I'm Ian," a short, red haired man said. I'm the farm manager for Willbourn Grange. My friend here is Wellington Willbourn." Wellington was a rather small, white haired man with a bushy beard and red face.

"You live at the grange?" I asked.

"Indeed I do, but I am the third son of his lordship's aunt," he said. "They can't throw me out, but they wish I wasn't there."

The men seemed to accept me as one of them and were unembarrassed at their nudity. Angus and Robert helped me undress as the other men embraced and groped each other.

I was erect by the time I was naked, but that didn't bother the men. Robert licked my cock as Angus straddled my face and fed me his member. His cock was wrapped in thick foreskin and wider than it was long. For a while, I thought he wasn't hard, but I soon realized the skin covered his cock head even when fully erect. I worked my tongue into the puckered skin end immediately encountered the fluid Ralph called cock jelly.

I licked around the tender head and Angus moaned in pleasure. I wouldn't have guessed that such a crude looking man would have been so sensitive, but my tongue caressing his knob drove him to distraction. The hot space between his cock head and the skin was flooded with new fluids as I licked. Much to my surprise, my tongue went to his piss slit and I licked up the fresh goo that oozed from his cock.

"Don't go too fast," he said as he pushed my head away. "We have the full day to play." Robert took his place. I had no idea what he would be like. From a distance, it was easy to think of him as an oddity or a curiosity. Close up he was very much a man.

While his legs were stunted, his trunk was heavily muscled and he indeed looked like a Classical statuette of Hercules. His genitals weren't at all classical. His cock was full sized, long, curved and very hard. I had just begun sucking him when I twisted the wrong way and I had a back spasm. Robert immediately moved and got me into a better position.

"You need a good rubdown," he said. "It will loosen you up."

"He's not good about relaxing," Ralph said. "Your rubdown will help him. I've got some oil that will help."

"I'll be all right in a minute or two," I said. "You don't need to bother." As seemed to be the case with Ralph, Robert didn't seem to be interested in my opinions. He rolled me on my stomach and poured some oil on my back. Next, he straddled me and rubbed the oil in.

Robert kneaded every muscle in my back. His hands and the oil seemed to get warm and I got less tense when I realized he knew what he was doing. I relaxed and came close to falling asleep. From my position on the bed, I could watch the other men frolic. My vision of an orgy was based on painting Roman orgys.

I had never imagined what an orgy with friends might be. Certainly, the air was filled with the scent of excited men, but they were no shy virgins, dreading the inevitable deflowering. The men here were sharing their bodies for mutual enjoyment. It was like a festive banquet among friends, except the men were feasting on their friends genitals rather than on food. As far as I could tell, each man offered up his privates as the price for sampling his friend's organs.

I fell asleep. When I woke, I was more relaxed than I had been in years. I felt euphoric and all was well with the world. Robert was still rubbing my back and I was deeply sexually excited. I was slightly dazed when I woke. It took a few moments to realize that while I slept, Robert had eased his cock into my ass.

Every time he rubbed my back, he had pushed his member deeper into me. Ralph and Wellington were watching me and had amused expressions on their faces. I should have been either embarrassed or shocked. I was neither.

I didn't know anything could feel that good. Truthfully speaking, I hadn't known a mere human could feel such heights of pleasure. I was sure his member was fully embedded in my ass and Robert was rocking forward trying to press deeper. He couldn't get deeper, but his efforts felt wonderful.

"Robert's a sly one, but I've never seen a man take it so well," Ralph said. I couldn't believe another man's cock was in my ass and I was enjoying it so much. The very thought should have been repulsive to me, but obviously, my body loved it. Robert slowly removed his member from my ass. For a few seconds he left the knob inside my hole, and then he pulled out.

Somehow I had the impression fucking was an ordeal to be feared. I should have been relieved it was over. The only feeling I actually had was of emptiness. It was as if I had found a void in my body that could only be filled with another man's cock.

Ralph seemed to understand. "Your back feels better now, doesn't it?" he asked.

I rolled over and smiled. "I've forgotten I have a back," I said. Alexander, the youngest man in the group next to me, came over to the bed. He lifted my legs to his shoulders and pushed his organ into my hole. It was as long as Robert's, but had more girth and a bigger knob.

I felt a twinge of pain as his knob popped into my ass. "Bobby warmed you up good," Alexander said as he pushed deep. "Real good." His cock head was in a few inches when a wave of intense pleasure all but overwhelmed me. I was in heaven. It was unbelievably intense. For the first time in my life I couldn't think. I could only feel.

I was naked in the midst of a group of men I had just met. They were fucking me in the ass and I was enjoying it. Oddly, I didn't seem to be worried about it at all.

I think the experience was so far beyond my range of experiences, I had no way to relate it to my life before this date. I had never seen a naked man until I saw Ralph the day before. I didn't know a man could take a cock in his ass. My knowledge of sex was primarily literary, not physical.

Ralph and his friends had no literary interests. Alexander began thrusting deep stokes and then stopped. I knew he was shooting his seed into me. He pulled out. The empty feeling returned. Wellington took Alexander's place. His cock was thin, but his head was large. The shaft was so thin, I only could feel the plum sized gland rubbing the insides of my ass.

"Damn!" he cried, "I've just drained my balls. I'm sorry Robert; I thought I could give you a better ride."

"We'll wear him out," Angus said. "Let him rest."

"Let me be the judge of that," I said. All the men laughed.

"He's a man after my own heart," Ian said. "You're a right randy lad, Robert. We're just as randy. There's about four feet of cock in this cottage, and you've only taken 18 to twenty inches of it. You can take it all, if you're game. Just tell us when you've had your fill, and we'll stop."

Ian was a wiry man, short of stature, but muscular. He had a pointed red beard and bright red hair covered his chest. He coated his cock in oil and eased it into my hole. He took his time. In the course of the next half hour, Ian introduced me to wide variety of sexual positions. Fucked me from the rear, doggy style and had me sit on it. He sat on mine, and had me fuck him doggy style.

Ian was the first man I had ever fucked. He wasn't open and I was afraid I might hurt him. Ian wasn't worried about that at all. He wanted me to force my way into his resisting body. I didn't think I could do that, but my cock had other ideas.

Once I got in, I started pounding him hard. He kept on crying," Harder, harder!" I couldn't stop. "Fill me up!" he cried.

I grabbed his shoulders and forced his body onto my bloated cock. It was as if I were shooting a rapid-fire rifle into his body. I shot volley after volley after volley. Ian was skewered on my cock and could do nothing but take my seed.

I almost feel asleep after my orgasm. I was in a daze. When my mind cleared, Ralph said, "That was beautiful!"

I looked at Ian to see if he was mad at me. I hadn't been gentle at all. He rolled me over and reinserted his member into my ass. He gently pumped, massaging the lining of my rectum. All was well.

"It's time to take a rest and eat something," Ralph said. He set out bread and cheese and had some beer. We talked as we ate. The fire warned the room as well as it could, but without the intense sexual activity generating body heat, the room began to feel chill. Fortunately, the rain and wind had abated outside.

There was a rapping at the door. Angus looked through a peephole and then opened the door. A tall, massive turbaned Indian entered the room. "Ram is here!" Ralph said, "I didn't think he could make it."

Ram wore the livery of a noble house. The men greeted him warmly as he stripped off his clothes. He was dark skinned with pitch-black hair. He was muscular and well put together. Silky, black hair covered his massive chest. His cock was his most outstanding feature. It looked larger than Ralph's huge member did. He was circumcised, so his gland was exposed. It was a beautiful shade of pinkish-lavender that contrasted with his dark skin.

CHAPTER 2

To say I was shocked at the Indian's arrival understates the case. I had never met an Indian before. Indeed, I had only recently met a Catholic for the first time. That man had been the most exotic person I had encountered in my white, Scots and Presbyterian life. A man from the moon would hardly have been more unexpected.

Not only was he an Indian, but he was also naked. The other men seemed to have no problem with him and he seemed to be both hearty and cheerful. His accent was more that of Oxford than of the sub-continent. As I watched him greet the men, his cock began to grow. I had guessed he was a bit larger than Ralph's impressive member was. I was wrong about that. It was much larger, being a foot or so long and impressively thick too. He was a big man, but I wondered how he supported the bloated member.

I soon discovered something quite unexpected. The massive organ seemed to have magnetic qualities. I had never considered the possibility of having intercourse with a man of another race. However,

I found my mind returning to thoughts of Ram's cock repeatedly. It seemed to cast a spell on me. At the time, I thought it was almost magical.

Now I realize it is more easily explained by my general interest in men and their cocks. Then, I was unwilling to believe I could have been motivated by such base interests. I thought of myself as living on a higher plane. How little I knew myself.

While I had been the center of attention before Ram appeared, he now took center stage. That was good for me. I had enjoyed the morning's couplings, but I was getting near my limit. I had been a virgin the day before. I could use a rest. I also wanted to watch.

I was always a good child who obeyed the rules. I had no idea what rules governed these men. I knew that in the world of Oxford rank and wealth governed all relations. I was wealthy, but my father had earned his knighthood, not inherited it. The boys from the upper tiers of the aristocracy didn't associate with the likes of me. Tristan was of minor gentry.

At Oxford, we talked about the plight of the worker, but did so without knowing any other than servants. I knew that some persons had relationships with persons of inferior rank. This was frowned upon and regarded as a flaw. Many of the boys treated their servants like dirt. In my ignorance, I assumed that these were merely social relations. I realized now the real sin was sexual relations.

I could understand the threat presented to an upper class couple if either strayed and found pleasure in lower class persons. My parents were a love match, but that certainly was an exception to the rule. In a loveless marriage undertaken for economic benefit, a house cleaner or servant would be great temptation. My father was a manly man, energetic and vital. He provided for our every need through his own labor and intelligence. We had no inherited wealth. When I met the languorous and pampered sons of the aristocracy, I could easily see their wives being attracted to a vital and muscular gardener or a groom.

There was a clear sense of democracy in my playmates in this cottage. It was a mutual assistance society. While some were more active than others were, all contributed to the pleasure of all. I noticed no one was left out. As the new man in the group, I had received much attention, but once I met them all, I was just a member of the group. Once you are naked, no one can tell you are a gentleman. Nude men can't hide their emotions. If you are excited, you get hard and there is no way to hide that. A spurting cock indicates an orgasm. That too can't be hidden. In this group, the only thing that counted was one's ability to give pleasure. My ass had certainly done that.

I would never have guessed that lying on a bed with men shoving their cock into my ass would give me so much pleasure, but it surely did. I knew it was pleasurable for them too, most were still drooling their man seed when they pulled out. As an added benefit, my back felt fine. I don't know if it was Robert's massage or the cocks that did it, but I was cured.

That afternoon I went seeking out cock. I started with Robert the dwarf. He had been the first man to fuck me and was the first man I sucked that afternoon. He had shot off already and I wasn't sure he would be able to shoot off again. I took his foreskin into my mouth, and then worked my tongue into the pucker. At first, I could taste soap faintly. Ralph had a washbowl available to clean up between sexual interludes. A second or two later my tongue caressed the delicate edge of the cock head where it joins the foreskin. Robert shivered a little when I did this. My tongue strayed to his slit and Robert rewarded me with some of his ball juices.

Since he had already climaxed, his organ grew slowly, so I had time to explore it in detail. His cock was long and thin. It was hard to take the entire thing until we got on the bed. When he sucked me and I sucked him at the same time, the curve of his cock matched perfectly the curve of my throat. The knob was large and flared at the edges. The edge was very sensitive, but not as sensitive as the area on the underside of the cock where a web of skin connected to the foreskin. Since it was directly below the slit, his cock juices drooled directly onto my tongue as I licked the tender spot.

I was licking that spot when rich and thick man cream spurted into my mouth. I shoved my tongue into the slit to dam up the flow. Robert moaned in pleasure as his seed built up, trapped in his organ. I relented and my mouth filled with an explosion of his seed.

I would have thought that I might have been repulsed as the dwarf's seed spurted into my mouth. I loved it. It was as if I received a reward for a job well done. He had been the first to enter my ass and open up a new world of pleasure for me. It seemed only fair to return pleasure for pleasure.

Many people talk of sex as if it consists of one person using another for his pleasure. That certainly was not my experience. As Robert pumped his seed into my mouth, I felt as if I were sharing his orgasm. I was almost as excited as he was and enjoyed it immensely.

"Why don't you go and sport with William, the Miller," Robert whispered once his ejaculations stopped. "He's shy, but thinks you are handsome. If you like my seed, you'll love his." I went over to the thin, small man. He was at the side or the room observing. William was perhaps five feet four. He was wiry, rather than muscular, like the stonemasons. I hadn't noticed him.

William was pale and smooth, unlike most of the men, but he had a thick bush of black hair. His cock seemed modest, but he had rather beautiful balls. They were the size of large hens' eggs and hung low in his sack. I reached over and fondled them. He looked up at me and smiled.

"The men like you," he said.

"Only half as much as I like them," I replied. "I didn't know I could enjoy men this much."

William smiled. "I know what you mean. I was brought up in a hard working, but somber and austere home," he said. "My father seemed to think physical pleasure was sinful. I have four brothers and three sisters. My mother died delivering a stillborn girl. Father thought that her death was the wages of sin for his lusty nature. When I chanced upon Ralph I thought I had landed in a foreign land filled with pleasure."

As I played with his balls his cock began to bloat, he continued to talk. I dropped to my knees and took the swelling organ into my mouth. As before, I felt great satisfaction. The hard cock was a testament to a job well done. While his organ quickly became fully erect, my own was not far behind.

"Your cock is beautiful," he whispered. "Do you think it would fit in my arse?" I looked up at him, unsure what to do. "I oiled my arse up already," he continued, "Work your finger in. I'm nice and open."

I didn't want to do this, but my natural desire to please triumphed. I had a hand holding his balls, so a moved a finger toward his hole. When I touched it, his cock spurted a glob of fluid. This tasted good, and I pushed my finger further. I found his ass pucker and pushed my finger through the tight sphincter.

He moaned in pleasure when I did this, the flow from his cock increased. He was more excited, but I was unexpectedly thrilled. All of a sudden, all my concerns about shoving my fingers up another man's behind vanished.

"Find the nut," he whispered. I pushed deeper and found a soft gland a few inches up his rectum. I pressed it and William cried in pleasure. I worked a second finger into the hole and squeezed it from both sides. William cried again. I was still sucking him, so I could taste his reaction. The sensations he felt were telegraphed to me though his oozing cock.

Somehow, a minute later my hard cock caressed the tender gland. I hadn't intended to screw him. I knew he wanted it and it seemed necessary. William more than loved it. I knew how my finger affected him. My cock generated double or quadruple the pleasure of the finger.

It seemed odd to me that my cock was so more pleasurable than my finger. My cock was much bigger than my finger, but the nut was just inside the ass. The finger reached it easily. My cock over shot it. Until a few days before, my cock had been an organ used to aim urine. I used it for my own pleasure late at night. I lived in fear someone would discover the sticky remains of my pleasure.

A few years later, I realized the cock was at the center of human existence. Without an erect and excited cock, all animal life would vanish. The intense pleasure I encountered with Ralph wasn't an oddity, or a perversion. It was the basis of life. In my solitary nighttime experimentation, the pleasure never approached what I felt with Ralph, or Robert or William. The pleasure was why men gather. I realized the pleasure was so intense, for most men the solitary life wasn't desirable.

In my polite life in England's minor gentry, the cock was non-existent. It was tolerated since one had to have an heir, but it was hidden from view and never mentioned. To mention the organ was all but forbidden. To see the forbidden organ was a sin and an abomination. Polite people were shocked and appalled. Here in Ralph's little cottage the men were unashamed of their bodies and of their organs. My head was spinning with all these new thoughts and revelations.

The party broke up in the late afternoon. I helped Ralph clean up. He made dinner; we ate, talked some, and then went to bed. It seemed cold in the cottage without the warmth of all the other men, but he stayed close to me. "You're a good man, Robert Fairbairn," he whispered. "The men liked you. They could tell."

"I liked them," I replied. "I didn't know you could feel what I was feeling. I didn't seem possible."

"You're lucky to discover that while you're still young," Ralph observed.

The next day a cart arrived to take me to Tristan's home. My back was fine. I bid Ralph a more than fond good bye and went with the carter. Tristan's home, called the Ramble, was a low, sprawling home of mismatched parts. Several parts looked Elizabethan, but the main part of the house was no more than a century old.

Inside, I discovered the house made up in comfort what it lacked in architectural coherence. I was greeted as a hero by Tristan's family, Lord and Lady Redborough and their two daughters. Tristan was still in bed recovering. Lord Redborough was slim and elegant, like Tristan. It took only a minute to realize her ladyship ran the place.

The girls were younger than Tristan, but very much the center of attention. I went to see Tristan. He looked weak. The break was more serious than I had thought. He was clearly uncomfortable, so I left and let him sleep. The family was preoccupied, so I took an opportunity to walk the grounds. The gardens were quite lush and well tended. I saw a gardener as asked about the other man who had been injured in the accident.

He said he was recovering. "Where does he live?" I asked.

"Virgil, he's in the cottage behind the dairy Sir," he answered.

"Would it be alright to visit him?"

"I'm sure it would, Sir. The dairy is over there, behind the summer house at the rear of the garden."

I went to the rear, found the dairy, and then found the cottage. I knocked on the door. A small woman answered.

"I'm Robert Fairbairn. I was in the carriage when your husband had the accident. I was just calling to see how Virgil was doing."

"Come in sir," she said. "He's right in here." I had to duck to get through the door. The inside of the house was small and crowded. Virgil was on a bed to the side of the room. He looked up.

"Oh, you're the gentleman who helped with the carriage," he said. "How is your back?"

"Quite recovered," I said. "You and Tristan took the brunt of the accident. How is your leg?"

"It's coming along," he said. I looked as he wife. She looked deeply worried.

"Has the doctor seen it?" I asked.

"It's not that bad," Virgil said. I wished him good luck and returned to the main house. I met the Butler at the door and asked if the doctor had seen Virgil.

"His Lordship rarely sends a doctor to the stable hands," the Butler replied.

"If the doctor visits could you ask him to visit Virgil? I asked. I slipped him several crowns. "I think the man is doing poorly."

"Certainly, kind Sir," he replied, "This will cover several visits." I went to the hall, where her Ladyship and the girls were talking.

"Your gardens are beautiful," I said.

"They are my pride and joy," she said, "Along with my children, of course. Mr. Fairbairn, I have a favor to ask of you. You are a guest, and let me assure you, you have every right to say no. I ask for a pure favor."

"Certainly, what do you wish?"

"My daughters are expected at a house party at our neighbor's, the Earl of Craigmiller. Tristan was to accompany them, but that is impossible. His lordship and I need to stay with Tristan. Could you accompany them? It's unseemly for them to travel unaccompanied by a gentleman. The girls have their hearts set on the party. The cream of society will be there."

I said I had hoped to spend some time with Tristan. They said he needed the rest. I agreed to accompany the girls. The next morning we set off in a carriage to visit the Earl's seat, Dunganon Castle. It was a long and bumpy ride. The road was poor.

Dunganon was a massive and impressive pile of stone, towers and turrets. When I got closer, I realized the house was modern. The Earl had an ancient title, but their wealth was modern. Lady Craigmiller's father owned coalfields in the Midlands. Her wealth paid for Dunganon Castle.

The Butler greeted us. Much to my surprise, Ram, the Indian from Ralph's, was the butler. Neither he, nor I gave any indication of having met. He took us to the Great Hall where the Earl's daughters squealed in excited greeting. The Earl had six daughters. All were pretty and all were loud. The girls laughed, squealed, and giggled. Behind the girls was Lady Craigmiller. She was an older copy of her daughters. Behind her, was the Earl himself. He was a tall and imposing man in a General's uniform. I recalled he had distinguished himself as an army commander in India. That explained the Indian Butler.

I was politely greeted, but since I am a quiet person, I was largely ignored. The Earl suggested I might walk in the gardens. "This is a hen house," he said. "The girls are plotting a way to snatch a suitable husband. The hope is to marry one of the Queen's grandsons, but that takes a lot of talk as you can well imagine! Men are entirely unnecessary here except to dance."

The landscape around the house was windswept, austere and stark. I thought it was beautiful and almost spiritual. I found a walled garden filled with beautiful flowers. The quiet was wonderful after the din inside the house. On the south side of the castle was large conservatory that grew exotic flowers and vegetables that were too tender to grow outside.

We had lunch in a small sun filled room. The Earl and I were the only males in the group and we were very extraneous to the excited conversations of the girls, their mother and a spinster aunt or two. Later the Earl showed me the library so I could find something to read. I went to my room in the bachelors quarter's of the house.

The house itself was well appointed, but the rooms for unattached males were Spartan and in a separate wing of the castle. The guests were to arrive the next day and the entire house would be occupied. For this night, I was the only resident of the wing. After dinner, the ladies went off to try on their dresses and make last minute alterations. I went to my room with my book.

I had been there for about a half hour when someone knocked on my door. I was an older man I recognized and the Earl's valet.

"I'm Billings, the general's man," he said. "It may be presumptuous to speak to you, but Ram told me you were a lusty lad who likes a bit of fun." He looked uncomfortable.

I smiled, "Ram is an impressive man," I said. "In many ways."

"That he is, without a doubt," Billings replied. "One way really tickles my fancy for sure. I'm not as impressive as he is, but I know how to have a spot of fun. Did you know there is a Turkish bath in the conservatory?"

"No I didn't," I said. I looked at Billings. He was older and had a white beard, but he looked ruddy and healthy. He was wearing the Earl's livery that had tight pants and I could see the outline of his genitals. He was either well endowed or partially erect.

"This place is private?" I asked.

"Don't you worry about that," Billing replied. "It isn't a place for shy men or for delicate types. The Maharajah said you would have no problem."

"Maharajah?"

"That's our name for Ram," he explained. I reached out and felt his growing bulge. He smiled and told me to follow him. We went down a rear stair and across a service yard to the back of an odd-looking building next to the Conservatory. It contained a boiler room. Walking around the equipment and the huge boiler, we came to a small door. Billings had a key. He flipped a latch to unlock the door and then locked it behind us.

We were in a handsome, wood paneled room. "Strip here, Sir," he said. He opened a concealed cabinet with hooks for clothes. As he was already half naked I followed suit. In the Earl's livery, he looked like a dandy. Naked he was all man. I was partially erect.

"Ram said you cut and impressive figure for a youth," he said as he stroked my cock. He pushed the skin back to fully expose the head. We then went through another concealed panel into the Turkish bath itself. The gas lighted room was tiled in beautiful colored designs. Blue, white and gold were the primary colors, but some rust and green added splashes of other hues. The air was thick with steam, so everything six feet or more away was veiled. In the middle of the room was a pool.

Walking around the pool we came to Ram, who was sitting on a throne like chair made of tile. A marble bench sat against the wall with many pillows. Billings walked up to Ram and then bent over and sucked his cock.

"I see you brought our guest," Ram said in his Oxford accent. His voice was very deep. "I admired you at the Smith's house. Ralph and I are friends and we share the same interests and affections. He sent me a note that I would enjoy you." Billings was still licking Ram's organ. When he got to us, the magnificent cock was still only half-erect. Billing was fully excited.

I moved forward to greet Ram, but I too bent over and began to administer to Ram. Apparently, that was the right thing to do. I could barely get the cock head into my mouth, but there was more than enough head to occupy my time. Ram was erect now. He held my head in his hands and played with my hair.

"I admire youth and youthful vigor, but I also like manly men," Ram whispered to me. "I don't like shy, frightened boys who are afraid of their shadows. Some men look at me and think I will rip them in half. You looked at me and realized the potential for physical pleasure. Ralph told me you had been a virgin the day before. I could tell the gods made you to give pleasure and to feel pleasure." I now could taste his sweet cock juices.

"Ram," A voice called out. "We have a new guest!" much to my surprise it was the Earl. Ram got up and surrendered the throne to the Earl. Billings came over and sucked his master's member.

"Mr. Fairbairn, I didn't expect to find you here, but I must confess to being pleased," the Earl said. "I live in a hen house, but I like to be with some cocks too." Billings rose from his master's cock and I took his place. "You are also unexpectedly well equipped. You sport a beauty. After all my years as a fancier of men, I still never know what's under the clothes. You are a find."

Ram was circumcised, but the Earl's member was fully hooded. Indeed, at first I thought he was all shroud without the body. I took the skin into my mouth. As my tongue probed deep into the tube of skin, I failed to encounter the organ. He was still soft. Billings' administrations had not excited him.

I soon found the tip of his knob and made it grow. It was a full sized tool, with a shroud two sizes too big. Protected by the encasing skin, the organ itself was tender and most responsive. I stood to catch a breath. The Earl stood too. He pulled his skin open and I slipped my cock into the tube. My knob met his knob. I felt a tickling sensation as he bathed my cock in his seed.

When I withdrew my cock from the Earl's foreskin, it was coated. Several men entered as we coupled. One of then came over and licked my cock clean. Another went to the Earl licked the remains of his orgasm from the inside of his skin.

"We only have two rules here," Ram whispered in my ear. "Nothing is forced, and no man seed is wasted. All are equal once you have greeted the chieftain."

"The Earl is the chieftain?" I asked.

"When he is in the chair, he is," Ram explained. "When he is on his feet, he is just one of the tribe."

"Whoever is in the seat, is the Chieftain?"

"Yes, that is the way it works." Ram explained. "Anyone can sit there, but mostly it is the Earl or me."

The man sucking my cock was blond, bearded, bull of a man. When he was finished, he stood.

"That was good," I said. "I am Robert Fairbairn."

"I'm Sean," he said. "I'm a farmer." He said that in a way that made me think he was a yeoman farmer, not a tenant. "It were my pleasure, sir," he added. "The Earl, he shoots a nice load. You're got a nice one too." I fondled his genitals and he looked pleased. Sean was a strong man; heavy work made him muscular.

CHAPTER 3

Sean's cock began to emerge from its sheath, so I bent over and licked it. His cock was a thick tube, and it may well have been wider than it was long. I licked his piss slit and tasted the first drop of his ball juices. His slit was wide so I flicked my tongue and worked my way into his shaft. He liked that. I stood up. "Very nice," I said. "You must stretch a man's hole wide open when you screw him.

"I love to top a man, but I don't get many takers," he said. He leaned close to me and whispered. "I don't mind getting plugged by a gentleman such as yourself. The Earl's shot so much seed in me; he says he's going to have to adopt me."

I smiled. "Have you taken the Indian's tool?"

"Well, I've drunk from the spigot often enough, but he's too big for me," Sean said. "Usually Ram feeds me his cock and holds me open while then Earl plows the field."

"Do other men plow the field?"

"I hope you wouldn't feel badly about me if I did?" he whispered. "Some think it's unmanly."

"I had a cock up my behind for the first time a few days ago," I said, "I didn't know anything could feel that good."

Sean smiled, "That's the way it struck me too, sir. I have seven boys, so I'm good at the other too, but the Earl and the other men here are different. It's pure joy."

A younger man walked by us holding a glass object. "Billy, come over here," he said, "This gentleman might need you." When the young man got closer, he looked slightly familiar.

"Billy, this is Robert, he's a guest of the Earl," Sean said, "Billy's the only one of my sons who likes it here."

That explained the resemblance. Billy was slimmer than his father was, but still solid and he had a golden beard, unmixed with white hair. Billy shared his father's smile too. He didn't seem to be bothered by his father's erection. He stoked my cock in greeting. He was half-hard when we met, but was at full staff a few seconds later.

"What are you carrying?" I asked.

"It's one of the Earl's inventions," Billy said. "You cover it in oil, then use it to slick up the love tunnel. When you oil up the cock, it makes it easy to take it up the back side." He showed it to me. It was seven or eight-inches long and was a curved, crystal tube with a bulbous tip. Seen close up it was clearly a cock. "The oil works well, but the tip also stretches open the hole too. Lie on the bench and I'll open you up."

I looked around. There now were perhaps ten or eleven men in the room. Several I recognized as members of the Castle staff, others I guessed were farmers. Billy must have sensed my unease.

"Don't worry," he said. "I've already oiled the Earl's behind, and Ram's." I got on the marble bench next to the wall. Billy dipped the bulbous end into a bowl of oil. I pulled my legs up and he oiled my ass. The implement was cool. He pumped it and after maybe thirty seconds it popped though my sphincter and into my ass. It was perfectly smooth and while it wasn't as exciting as a man's member, it was good.

Billy played with it for a while then took it out. He dipped it in the oil again and went in for a second time getting oil deeper in my rectum. He took it out again. This time he dipped his cock in the oil and slipped it into my ass.

After the cool crystal, the hot cock attached to the excited farmer's son was more than pleasurable. Billy wasn't quite as thick as his father was, but he was longer. He was still talking informally as he pumped my hole. The Earl passed by.

"I hope you like the hospitality of the Castle?" he asked. "This is just about the only place you can get away from the girls. I love them dearly, but it's good to get to a sanctuary away from them."

"It's all I could wish," I said. "I didn't expect this at all." Billy pulled out and the Earl took his place. He easily worked his long and thick cock into my ass. He liked long deep strokes.

"I hope it doesn't shock you, Mr. Fairbairn, the Earl said. "I have the misfortune of having potent seed as well as the sex drive of a bull. Almost every time I plowed the marital field, I seem to have a daughter nine months later. After six daughters, I realized my wife would be dead if I didn't find another outlet. I chanced upon Ram while stationed in India. With him I discovered an alternative."

"Was he your servant?" I asked.

"Not at all, we were cell mates," he explained. "I was captured in an ambush while traveling alone and was thrown into a vile prison where I found Ram. He was the son of the neighboring Maharajah and the bandits were holding him for ransom."

"This is a story from a Kipling adventure!" I exclaimed.

"Indeed, but the story isn't over," the Earl said. "Ram was the second son, and much more of a man than his weaker older brother. The heir had no desire to pay the ransom. The bandits planned to chop off a few of his extremities to inspire more prompt delivery of the money. He was in a dire situation."

"It was a hot cell and they weren't going to feed us, or get us water. Some Indians have no problem drinking piss as a religious exercise. Ram took mine. Soon, I was so desperate, I took his. I was prepared to be sickened, but I was titillated. I enjoyed it and when his flow diminished, I continued nursing his cock until I got some of the cream. Most men's seed would provide only a few drops, but Ram is a stallion and I got a full mouthful."

"Ram returned the favor. In that dismal cell, these daily explosions of pleasure were a delight. Neither Ram nor I are fools. We realized we liked, and indeed loved, the sexual connection. We felt no need to claim imprisonment to justify it in our own minds. Food and water are important, but an orgasm or two a day lifts the spirits."

"How did you escape?" I asked.

"They left us alone most of the day and we played as if we were near death. When they sent an underling to check on us, we overpowered him and got out. Fortunately, while my unit had given up the hunt for me after two weeks, they were still concentrating their patrols in the approximate area of my disappearance. We were no more than two miles from our place of captivity when we found them."

"And Ram stayed with you?"

"He understood the abduction had spared his brother from the trouble of having him murdered. He was safer with me," the Earl explained. "This also gave us an opportunity to further explore the pleasures of man to man sex. As an Indian prince, he had much more knowledge on this subject than I did. Everything in the kingdom was available for the ruler's sexual pleasure, man, woman, animal or vegetable, for that matter."

"We are lucky Queen Victoria is so restrained," I said.

The Earl continued fucking me as he told the story, changing the pace and depth of his trusts to punctuate the high points of his tale. When I mentioned Queen Victoria, he laughed and gave me a hard, trio of thrusts. He suddenly became rigid as a board as he diverted his energies to shooting his aristocratic seed into my gentrified ass.

He relaxed. "Mr. Fairbairn, that was quite wonderful. We must do this again."

"Thank you," I replied as he left.

Sean and Billy had watched the scene. "That was lovely," Sean said. He slipped his thick tube of meat into my just vacated hole. I opened wide and it was painless. "I like my sex like a barn yard animal," he said. "Would that bother you?"

"Give it a try," I said. He began thrusting like a mad man. In a short time, he too had deposited his seed in my ass.

"That was good, sir," he said as he pulled out. I got off the bench. It seemed as if anyone passing by felt the urge to fuck me. That was fine, but I wanted to see who else was in the room. I went to the pool. Ram was in the water talking with a black haired, bearded man. A younger lad sat next to me.

He leaned near me. "I've never been here before," he said.

"It's my first time too," I said. "My name is Robert."

"I'm Rob," he said. "I work in the boiler room. I'm a stoker." Rob had pale, white skin, and hair beginning to grow around his tits and in the middle of his chest. A tail of hair connected to his very think bush. His uncut cock peaked out of the thicket of hair. He did not impress you as being muscular, but when you looked at him closely, you realized he was strong. He was obviously uncomfortable and his cock was soft. He shivered a little. The room was very warm so it was nerves. I put my arm around him.

"Your work makes you strong," I said. He snuggled closer.

"It's hard work, but I've got no problem with that," he said. "My mum says I'm a regular work horse."

"Are you from here?"

"No, I'm from Leeds," Jack replied. "I was apprenticed to a boiler maker, but he was a bad man and I ran away. Big Jack found me and gave me a job here."

I glanced at the black haired man talking with Ram. "Is that Big Jack?"

Rob nodded. "A kinder man there has never been," he said. Some men in Rob's position pour praise on their masters to curry favor. I sensed Rob's affection was real. "He said he always wanted a son. He's taught me a lot."

"Has he taught you about man play?"

"That he has," Rob said with some enthusiasm. He leaned close to me and whispered. "Truthfully speaking I knowed some things about having a good time, before I came here. Big Jack says I got a good cock, but a better arse!"

Big Jack and Ram were both erect and I saw Big Jack had a massive member. "Did it fit?"

Rob smiled. "Not at first," Jack said. "It took some work, but it was worth it. He said once I'd taken his, any other cock would be easy." I had my arm around him and was rubbing him gently. His cock was growing.

"Can I ask you a question?" he whispered. I nodded. "I've sucked and been fucked right regular. Do you think anyone here would suck me? I've never been sucked."

"Have you ever fucked a man?" I asked.

Rob shook his head. I got in the water and took his cock into my mouth. He looked shocked, but I tasted some of his ball juices immediately. I also faintly tasted soap. It would take a lot of scrubbing to clean up a stoker. I guessed Big Jack made sure he was presentable to the group.

"He may have a hair trigger, Sir," a deep voice said. "Rob you make sure you tell him when you're going to pop. The gentleman may not want your cream." I looked up and saw the hulking figure of Big Jack. He was smiling. Big Jack's massive member was at eye level. His purple knob had almost peeled back the skin.

"I hope I'm not trespassing," I said.

"His apprenticeship is almost done," Big Jack said. "He's a good and lusty lad. Jack likes his fun. By the way, his cream is fresh, I milked him yesterday."

"Do you like the cream?" I asked as I licked Big Jack's knob.

"Never been much to my taste, sir," Big Jack said. "I fuck the cream out of him." I licked some juice that dribbled from Big Jack's slit, then returned to Rob's more modest member. It didn't take long to taste the creamy product of his balls. Rob looked as if he had died and gone to heaven. I sucked until I drained the last drop of his seed from his balls.

Once he had climaxed, Rob needed some recovery time so I left him alone. I joined Ram and Big Jack.

"The boy's happy, Big Jack said. "He wanted that bad. I think you gave him exactly what he wanted."

"I enjoyed it," I said. I looked around the room. There must have been fifteen men there. "I had no idea there were so many men like us."

Ram smiled. "Men are men everywhere. You can pretend they have no sexual urges, or you can suppress them, but they are always there," he said. "I noticed you are a generous man at Ralph's cottage. You must have an unconventional streak in you."

"I am afraid I am very ordinary," I replied. He fondled my cock. I had been playing with Big Jack's. I had two hands, so I could serve them both.

"You are an upper class boy who was thrown into a group of common men. This was all new to you, but you accommodated them well. You treated them like men, not servants, and you opened your body to them."

"Is that unusual?" I asked. "I know it is, but I was carried away by the moment."

"Well. Here you are a few days later, and you are with common folk again. Two farmers and an Earl have fucked you. Then you drained a boiler stoker's balls," he observed. "You aren't doing it to shock your father or your friends or to prove a political point are you?"

"I don't know why I'm doing it," I confessed.

"I think you do it because you take men at face value without the screen of class or wealth," Ram said. "I also think you are a naturally generous man. You offer your body for others' pleasure without expecting return."

"But I get enjoyment in return," I said.

"Of course you do," Ram said. "That is the result of your openness. Men want to please you out of a sense of fairness."

"I think you just a randy lad!" Big Jack proclaimed. Ram and I both laughed.

"You may have hit that nail on the head," I said. Someone called for Ram and he left.

"Let me introduce you to some of my mates," Big Jack said. "Let me warn you in advance. Earnest is deaf, so he may seem simple. He likes men and he likes to please. Now, Jelly is a bit simple. He's strong as an ox and can do anything you ask him as long as it doesn't take much thinking. Rob is the genius in the group. Eventually he can replace me. By the way, I cleaned them up real good for tonight. Everything is cleaned and polished."

Jelly and Earnest were in a corner watching the activity. When they saw Big Jack, their faces lit up. Jelly was huge; he could easily have been a boxer or circus strongman. He was smooth, but with a ruddy completion. He spent most of his life outside the castle. His face would have been handsome, but his eyes seemed dull.

Earnest was much smaller and about as hairy as man could be without being a monkey. I remember having been shocked when I first heard of Mr. Darwin's Evolutionary theories. When you saw Earnest, you realized how right Darwin was.

Big Jack put his arms around Jelly and said, "Jelly, this is Mr. Robert. He's a gentleman." Jelly smiled, but I think it was because Big Jack had embraced him.

"Mr. Robert," Jelly repeated. It sounded as if it were a foreign name to him.

Big Jack waved at Earnest to come over. "Mr. Robert," he said very loudly. Earnest looked at Big Jack's mouth.

"Rah Bert," he said a few times. "Oh, Robert," he said when he figured it out. He wasn't good looking. His face was lopsided and he had several scars. His back was scared, the sign of a bad beating. His eyes were a beautiful shade of pale blue. When I looked in them, they were like a deep pool of clear, still water. They were quite lovely.

I blinked and he blinked. He was looking into my eyes as I looked into his. He stroked the hair in my chest. "Hairy." he said.

I stroked his chest and said, "Very hairy." It took him a second, but he burst out laughing. I reached down and played with his equipment. It was hard to find in the hairy thicket of his pubes, but once I found it there was a lot there.

"Beautiful," I said. He smiled. I was at about half-staff. He stroked it and pulled the skin back from my cock head.

"Very beautiful," he said. I laughed. He began sucking me, but soon we were on the floor, sucking each other. Talking was a chore for Earnest, but his cock did all the communicating we needed. He had a bulbous, but rather small cock head, but his shaft was like an ancient oak with a huge base that tapered as it reached skyward. He had goat balls, large and low hanging. While the head was small, the slit all but bisected it and his balls kept a constant flow of sweet juices. After a while, he took my hand and directed it to his ass; he wanted to be fucked.

Earnest wanted me to sit on the marble bench. When I did, he sat back on my cock. I held him in place and spread his legs. Ram saw us and he sucked Earnest's cock. Then he sucked Earnest's balls and then my balls, dangling behind. This was very good for me and Earnest. Much to my surprise, he lifted Earnest up so he could lick my entire shaft.

We got on the floor, and Earnest impaled himself again, again with his back to me. Earnest leaned back and Ram began to lick the portion of my cock that wasn't in Earnest's hole. He was trying to get his tongue into the hole with my cock. Earnest went crazy with excitement. He shot off and Ram took the cream. I looked at Ram and he smiled. The deaf man's seed filled his mouth.

A minute later, Ram sat on the bench and I impaled myself on his monster. I was so aroused, only Ram's cock would do. It was huge and it wasn't easy, but much to my surprise it wasn't that hard either. Once half of it was in I was so far gone, the remainder wasn't a problem. I spread my legs as Earnest had done, and the sensations doubled. Every movement I made, no matter how slight was intensely pleasurable. It was lovely.

Big Jack joined us, licking and sucking our genitals and especially the place where Ram's cock entered my ass. It was too much for me. Big Jack's black beard looked as if he had been in a snowstorm. It was coated in my seed.

CHAPTER 4

By now, it was getting quite late, and I retired to my bedroom. The next day would be busy for the men, preparing the house for the ball. The first guests arrived at noon and were greeted by the Earl and his excited daughters. I saw Sean and Billy hauling luggage to the bachelor's quarters. There weren't enough footmen and household servants to handle the load. The guests were all well connected and wealthy. I did note that none of Queen Victoria's grandsons attended. I suspected the Earl was smiling inwardly.

I was of course invited to the ball, but I begged off. I didn't have my formal attire, and I said I might prefer to spend the night reading. Out of politeness, her ladyship begged me to come anyway, but when I demurred and reminded her of my back problem. She said she understood and looked slightly relieved.

I knew one or two men I knew from College. I told them about the accident and Tristan's misfortune. I was with one of Tristan's sisters and she told them about my bravery in trying to lift the wheel to free Tristan. "Were there no footmen?" Lord Cloverton asked. I knew Cloverton slightly. He was a pleasant fellow, but I realized he simply could not visualize traveling without a retinue.

The Earl took me aside in the library during a quiet interlude in the afternoon. "You are a handsome lad and a good sport to boot," he said.

"I enjoyed meeting you last night," I said. "It was a pleasure."

"Let me assure you, the pleasure was all mine," he said. The Earl leaned close to me and whispered.

"Ram enjoyed you too. He is always seeking out new experiences and you provided him with one last night. He was much impressed. Ram told me you are new to the sport?" I noted the Earl's conversation would see entirely innocuous to anyone who chanced to hear us.

"I am," I replied. "I played for the first time four days ago."

"You are lucky," he observed. "I wish I had learned to play when I was your age. By the way, Lord Annandale is here with his daughter Annabelle. He injured his foot on the trip here and will not attend the ball."

I didn't know why he mentioned this, and then I understood. "Is Lord Annandale a sportsman?" I asked.

"Oh yes," he replied. "A great sportsman. He is injured, but he can still play. I put him in a suite away from the noise of the ball. It is quite quiet and secluded there. I can tell him you might visit him to pass the time, if you're interested?"

"That would be nice," I answered. The Earl smiled. Three carriages arrived and the house resumed its normal character, noisy and confused. Most of the guests arrived between four and five and the place was in an uproar. There was light refreshment available, but the main dinner would be at 11:00 at the ball. The bachelor's quarters were over flowing with men and servants. By 8:30, it quieted down, as everyone was dressed. I returned to my room and found a plate of food and wine. Someone had remembered I wasn't going to the ball.

Shortly after all the guests went to the ballroom, someone knocked on my door. I opened it.

"Mr. Fairbairn?"

"Yes?"

"I'm Lord Annandale's man," he said, "I am to take you to his quarters. If you wish." The man was my Father's age. However, was dressed in Lord Annandale's livery. He wore tight pants in the 18th century style and I saw they barely contained his impressive equipment.

"Come in while I get my coat," I said, "I'd be happy to meet his Lordship."

He came in my room and closed the door. "Not half as happy as he will be," he said with a wink.

"I'm Robert Fairbairn."

"Cox here," he said. "Valet and all purpose man to his Lordship."

"And a lot of cock I see," I said looking at the bulge in his pants.

"I see you're a connoisseur," he replied. I put on my coat and we went to Lord Annandale's rooms. His Lordship was a handsome man and rather younger than I had expected. He was on the bed and had been drinking. While we were talking, he slipped to his side and began to snore. Cox came over and put a pillow under his head.

"The Doctor gave him a powder for the pain," Cox said. "I'm afraid he should have mixed it with water, not whiskey."

I laughed. "Does this happen regularly? I asked.

"Not at all. This is a first," Cox replied. "He will be very embarrassed tomorrow morning."

"Do you share his taste for entertainment?" I asked.

Cox looked me in the eye. "That I do, Sir," he replied. "His Lordship likes them younger than me, so I don't get much fun. Luckily I like to watch."

I stepped closer to him and cupped his impressive equipment in my hand. He looked at me and winked.

"Perhaps I could wait for him to wake up," I said. By that time, his hand was in the front of my trousers, searching for my genitals.

"That would be nice Sir," he said as he began to take off his clothes. Lord Annandale's livery was pale green satin with masses of white lace and the family crest embroidered on the waistcoat. There was a powdered wig too. Cox transformed himself from being a pop in jay to a ruddy worker as he stripped. He had shocking red hair and a heavy coat of red hair on his body. He reminded me of an orangutan I once saw in a zoo.

His skin was white but he had pink tits and a huge, pinkish-purple cock head poking out of his foreskin. I dropped to my knees and easily coaxed it to life out of the shroud.

"I didn't expect this," he said, "but the attention is more than welcome. Let's go to the bed where we can share better." Cox rolled his master to the side. When we got on the bed, he sucked me as I sucked him. He seemed to be hungry and swallowed my entire member. I tried to do the same for him and was surprised when I succeeded. From this angle, it fit my mouth. His shaft was thinner than his knob, and curved in a way that made it easy to swallow.

When I pulled off his organ to get a breath, I suctioned some of his man juices from his balls. Once I discovered the secret to getting his juices, I milked him. I was so excited by this I hardly noticed he was milking me. I had a feeling of almost goodwill as we shared our manly juices.

He pulled off. "Can I ask you a question, Mr. Fairbairn?"

I said surely.

"Would it bother you if I shot my load into your mouth? You're a gentleman. Some don't like a common man's seed," he asked.

"I like man seed," I said. "I'm not so sure there is much difference between a common man's balls and those of an aristocrat."

"Lord Annandale thinks there is," Cox said. "He'll feed me his, but not take mine. He likes to breed me like a dog."

"Does that offend you?"

"Not at all, truthfully speaking," he answered. "He's got a long, thin one that fits easily and feels good. It sort of tickles. He can also stay hard for hours. Once and a while I'd like to fuck a man."

"When did you get to do this?"

"The last time was when we visited the Earl. He's a fine man and neither he nor his friends put on airs. I had a great time in the Turkish bath."

"Were you here with Lord Annandale?"

"His lordship was there and he had a good time," Cox said. "He let the Earl and the Earl's men have their way with him, but not me, nor anyone from our house. The Earl seemed to take all who had a mind to." As he talked, he moved a finger toward my hole. When I didn't object, he licked his finger and returned it to my ass. He continued to talk as his finger pressed deeper.

"I had never seen him take it until the Earl popped him," Cox said. "Up to that time, I thought his arse was virgin, but he took the Earl's big thing easily." By now, his finger found my nut and I sighed in pleasure. He massaged the small gland.

"I see everything in your arse is in working condition," he said as he played with the gland. "I was really surprised when he took the Indian Giant's monster. It slid in his ass like a hot knife through butter. His Lordship likes to be in charge, but he was the Indian's cock slave the second the member was on the dark side of the arse."

Cox moved again. He spit on his cock and then spit into my hole. Then he spread my legs wide and nuzzled his cock head into my hole. "This may sting a little when I pop you, but it will feel great when I'm in," he said. He was in quickly. Cox was both forceful and gentle. I knew he would penetrate me, but he seemed almost relaxed and casual about it. There was a quick twinge of pain when the bloated tip of his cock entered, but then my ass closed on his thin shaft. I felt the odd sensation that his cock head alone was in my ass.

The bulbous knob explored my rectum. The sensations were unexpectedly pleasurable. He continued to talk. Cox was an amusing man and had many curious tales to tell. The sensations in my ass began to intensify as he continued his slow movements. By now, he had propped my legs on his shoulders and was stoking my cock. He spit on his hands to lubricate my cock.

"You got a beautiful one," he said as he stoked my member. "Sometimes the big ones aren't that pretty. I like them big, mind you, but some are just tubes of man meat. Yours is big and pretty, lovely head, thick shaft, nice ripe balls."

He let my legs down, straddled me and then sat on my cock in lightening like quick movement. My cock slid into his ass. He moaned in pleasure as he skewered himself. Once it was in, he sat still for a few moments, and then he began to bounce on my cock. He bounced three or four times. I filled his ass with my seed. When he was done, he got off my cock and fed me his cock. My tongue barely touched the tip of his cock when he unloaded the entire contents of his balls in my mouth.

"You're a good lad," he said. I was tired and went back to my room. The ball was still underway. I slept well. When I woke the next morning, the revelers had just gone to bed. I, with the servants, was the only one stirring. That afternoon I returned to Tristan's house with his daughters. The party had been a success and the girls had selected their future husbands. The gentlemen in question knew nothing of their good luck, but the girls amused themselves with fantasies.

At the Ramble, Lord and Lady Redborough greeted the girls as conquering heroes. Tristan was much better. As they entered the house, the doctor was leaving.

"I hear that Tristan is recovering," I said. "I am Robert Fairbairn, a friend of his from Oxford."

"Dr. MacEwan here," he said. The doctor was a distinguished looking man. "He is well on the way to full recovery. I'm afraid he may get suffocated from the attention lavished on him."

"They do dote on their children," I said.

He smiled. "By the way, you were quite right about Virgil. He was in a bad way. I cleaned out the infection and gave his wife instructions how to keep it clean. He has turned the corner."

"I'm pleased. When I visited him I didn't get a good feeling."

"It strikes me as odd that while the Redborough's are kindly they seem to have a blind spot in some areas," the Doctor said.

"Perhaps they were preoccupied with Tristan?"

He looked me in the eye. "You are a man who is liberal and generous in his attitudes and sentiments," he said. I understood he thought I was being kind rather than realistic about my hosts. "I greatly appreciate that, you have done a great service to Virgil." We shook hands and he left. I went to see Tristan who did indeed look better. I told him about the Earl's party. He enjoyed that, but was scandalized I had not attended the ball. I assured him I enjoyed myself.

I was surprised to note the servants seemed to be more differential to me. When I walked in the gardens, the gardeners tipped their hats to me and in the house, the maids curtsied. At dinner I noticed my meat was particularly choice, and wine glass was never empty. Lord Redborough mentioned I seemed to be quite the servants' pet.

My visit came to an end when I received a telegram from my father saying my Aunt had died and I had to be at the funeral in two days. He asked that I get there quickly and said he would bring my mourning attire with him. I was off on a horse to the nearest train station in two hours. My visit to Tristan had not been what I had expected it to be, but it was rewarding in many other ways.

I am a cautious traveler so I always allow extra time to insure I am on time. As I passed Ralph's cottage, I stopped to talk with him. He was hard at work, but was glad to see me. I told him of my time with Tristan and of my visit to the Earl.

"The Earl is a right randy gentleman, isn't he?" he said. He winked at me. "It is a friendly house." clearly he knew about the Turkish bath.

"That it was," I observed. I told him of my adventures there. "Might I visit you again sometime?" I asked.

"I would like that," he said. "You enjoyed the party?"

"I did, but I enjoyed the night before the party even more."

"I was thinking that too," he said. I had to get on my way. We kissed and I left. I got to the funeral and then spent some time at home with my father before returning to the University. I felt more mature and my friends, who I had looked up to the year before, seemed younger. I now understood they weren't that knowledgeable.

Several months later. The Earl visited Oxford and he had been a member of my college. I saw him in the quadrangle and he came over to speak to me.

"Mr. Fairbairn, it's good to see you. I knew you were here, but had no idea you went to my college," he said. What chatted and exchanged pleasantries. One of his daughters was engaged to the son of a Duke, so his wife was happy. "By the way, I going to visit an old friend here for dinner tonight, you might enjoy meeting him. We all share some common interests."

"I would hate to impose on a private party," I said.

The Earl smiled. "Don't give that a moment's thought," he said as he leaned closer to me. "The gentleman is a sportsman, like us." I agreed to go with him. I had no experiences since I left the Earl's castle four months earlier. Logically I should have realized there were men in Oxford who shared my interests, but I couldn't conceive of a way to meet them, so I put the idea out of my mind.

That evening, the Earl met me at the college gates in a carriage. Ram was with him as were Billy, Sean's son, and Rob, the stoker. We drove to a small, house on the edge of town. A tall, heavily bearded man greeted us warmly. He introduced himself as Edmund Bannister, but I knew him as Sir Edmund, noted botanist and famous explorer.

Two men were with him. Unexpectedly, one was Lord Cloverton, who I met at the Earl's house party, and the other was a huge, bruiser of a man named Ronnie.

Apparently, Sir Edmund knew Ram and Billy already. He greeted them warmly. Rob and I were new to him and he was more than cordial. I thought the house was small at first, but I realized it was new and well appointed. I don't know if a place can be modestly luxurious, but that would describe it well. It was very different from the showy mansions that distinguish our times.

Sir Edmund and Ronnie served drinks. Apparently, Ronnie was Sir Edmund's man, but there was no sense of the normal servant-master relationship. Ronnie addressed Lord Cloverton as Robin, and Robin gazed on Ronnie as if he were a god. I tried to visualize Ronnie and the rather delicate Robin coupling, but I couldn't.

One more man joined our group, Isaac Woolrich. He was an archaeologist famous for his Mesopotamian expeditions. He was a bearlike man with a white beard. Woolrich was much taken by Rob.

The room was low and a fire in huge fireplace warmed it in no time. It was furnished in oriental rugs and pillows on benches, chairs and divans. There was a slightly oriental air about the place that co-existed well with the English character of the house itself. I was chatting with Ram when I saw the Earl and Billy disrobing on the other side of the room. Ronnie was stripping Robin next to the fireplace. Isaac was with Jack.

Sir Edmund took me under his wing. He put his arm around my shoulders. "Are you a shy man?" he asked.

I smiled at him. "No sir," I said. "Not at all."

"Does it bother you to feed from the cock of a man you've just met?" he asked. I dropped to my knees and unbuttoned his pants. A minute later, we were both naked. Sir Edmund was sitting on a chair, and I was sucking his cock.

Robin, Lord Cloverton, was moaning on the other side of the room. He cried out, "Stop! Stop! I can't take any more." A second or two later he'd beg, "Get it deeper. Go all the way." I assume Ronnie was the man going deeper. However, I was too occupied with Sir Edmund to look up.

CHAPTER 5

I thought sex with a group of academics might be more delicate and refined than that with working men. I soon realized Sir Edmund and Isaac Woolrich were interested in sex as sex, pure and simple. Sir Edmund began to suck me the second we were naked. He wanted to fuck and he wanted to be fucked. Isaac had the same interests. Their interest in sex was very uninhibited. For them fondling a man's genitals or taking a cock in the ass was as ordinary as shaking hands, or hugging a dear friend.

"The highest expression of human existence is the ability to feel pleasure," Sir Edmund explained as he fondled my balls. "And no human pleasure can equal that generated by the genitals. There are those who talk of spiritual love and platonic relations, but as far as I can tell, they are little more than fairy tales."

"Some have a fear of pregnancy. Child bearing is wondrous and terrifying, creative of a child, but often destructive of the mother," he continued, "but when your partners in the sexual experience are all men, your mates and pals, there is no limit to the pleasurable potential."

I looked around the room as he spoke. Robin sat in Ram's lap. Ram held his legs up so Ronnie had full access to Lord Cloverton's ass. I hadn't seen Ronnie's tool, but it must have been long. The frantic begging that had marked the initial penetration was now replaced by a slow moaning. Beside me, the Earl was on his hands and knees. Billy was screwing him doggy style.

Isaac and Rob joined us. They were both erect.

"Have you been giving our young friend a lecture on the pleasures of sex?" Isaac asked. He had an amused look on his face. "Rob doesn't need a lecture. He can feel it." Isaac bent over and licked Rob's member.

"Rob's a child of nature," Sir Edmund whispered in my ear. "You are a proper English gentleman. It's hard for you to feel without guilt."

"What do you mean?"

"You have been warned that the pleasures of the flesh are sinful and evil," he explained. "A stiff upper lip, being true to your class, propriety and good manners are all barriers to our true nature. We suppress our natural inclinations and hide them from view."

"Can-not our natural inclinations lead us astray?" I asked. Sir Edmund put his arm around Rob and me. Isaac dropped to the floor where he could minister to all three cocks. It may seem childish, but I was proud I had the biggest of the three cocks. Sir Edmund had girth, but not length. It was a hard and solid tube of flesh. Rob was average in size. Isaac seemed to like all three of the organs and didn't show any favoritism.

Isaac looked up at me and I knew I was supposed to take his place. I was game. Isaac had a long cock of moderate girth. He head was big, but not huge. His balls were big. At first, I thought he wasn't fully erect, since his cock drooped. He was hard as steel. His cock curved in the opposite direction from mine. From this angle, I could swallow the entire thing. There was no urge to choke or gag. It was a perfect fit. When my nose was buried in his bush, I swallowed a few times. Isaac's cock twitched, but he didn't shoot.

"That's a beautiful sight," Sir Edmund said. "Does it feel as good as it looks?"

"Oh yes," Isaac said.

I slowly pulled away and moved on to Sir Edmund's meat. There was no way I could swallow his. I had been able to do it when I had first sucked him, although even then it had been a mouthful. Now he was fully erect. I opened my mouth wide to take the head. It was a beautiful shade of bluish lavender. He had been leaking man juice and the light of the fire sparkled in the quivering drool. When I got the head in my mouth, my tongue sought out the slit. The cum slit was wide as was the tunnel. Instead of licking the slit, I tongue fucked it.

I don't know how deep in the shaft I got, but it seemed deep. My lips held the tender flared edge of his cock head and my tongue pushed into the shaft. He was moaning. I moved on to Jack, but he was gone. Turning my head, I saw he was feeding at Isaac's cock. He had watched me take it all and was trying to do the same. I returned my attention to Sir Edmund's organ. All was well.

The evening was somewhat like a game of sexual musical chairs. We all admitted our interests and Sir Edmund and Isaac's lack of shyness was contagious. After an extended period of play, Ronnie brought out drinks and cakes. I had been so preoccupied by the sex; I hadn't realized I was hungry.

"Unless I am very mistaken we seem to be a most congenial group," Sir Edmund remarked. "I have been in few groups of this size before. Everyone is willing and open to the possibilities. I confess to being intrigued by the opportunities for shared orgasms, and multiple penetrations. I assume Ram and the Earl have some knowledge of the Indian classic Kama Sutra. I have never shared an ass with another man's cock. I have never screwed a man when I was being screwed. Do any of you share my interests?"

"You know damn well I'm interested," Isaac said. "I have wanted to be in a daisy chain of men, linked cock to mouth in a circle of lust. I want to know if the pleasurable sensations are amplified by multiple participants." Each member of the group expressed interest and willingness. I wondered if Billy and Rob would want to participate. Rob suggested the chain might consist of men linked cock to ass.

He glanced at me when he said this. I knew he wanted to fuck and this arrangement would insure his cock spent some time in the warm recesses of at least one or two of the men.

"I'm a top man," Ronnie said in his deep bass voice. "But in the interest of scientific inquiry," He winked at Sir Edmund when he said this. "I'd be willing to open up my hole for one of you, or all of you for that matter."

"Ronnie, you are a true gentleman and scholar," Isaac said mock seriously. "Is there anyone here who would be willing to contribute their mouths, cocks and asses to this scientific inquiry?" He raised his hand and every man in the room raised his hand at the same time.

"I'd love to screw every man in this room and feel every man's cock in my hole," Ram said.

"I'm not sure you'll fit in mine," Rob cried. Everyone laughed.

"You'll know soon enough," the Earl said. He got on the floor and got Rob next to him. He took the young stoker's cock into his mouth and began to suck with obvious relish. In a minute, we formed an irregular ring on the Persian carpet on the floor. I was on the floor sucking Ronnie as Robin sucked me. Ronnie had a club cock. The head was the same size as the shaft and was perfectly straight. It was seven or more inches long, the head was deep red, and so hard I could see my refection in it. It had been in Robin's ass, but it tasted only of Ronnie's man juices. I smelled only the musky man smells of his bush and bull balls.

Until I encountered Ronnie's balls, I thought of balls as a minor accessory to the manly scepter. His balls were the size of small apples or large eggs. They hung low and were heavy with man seed. I had hardly begun appreciating them when Sir Edmund called out and told us to switch partners. I rotated and took Robin's cock as Ronnie took mine.

I didn't find Robin particularity attractive, but in the spirit of the moment, I did what I could. His cock was smaller, but it was easy to take in its entirety. This I enjoyed. Ronnie enjoyed my cock with evident relish. He let a finger wander toward my ass hole. I shifted my leg to give him better access.

I moved my finger toward Robin's ass. He greeted the movement with obvious enthusiasm. His ass was already lubricated and my finger penetrated deeply. I inserted another finger. I continued sucking as my finger pushed and his cock began to drool profusely. My finger must have touched the prostate gland as Ronnie's thick digit pressed mine. It seemed as if we united in pleasure.

I soon realized Robin was fingering Jack and Jack did the same to his neighbor. We were now linked mouth to cock and finger to prostate. After a short while, Ronnie began to slide up against my back. I shivered in anticipation that his cock would soon be nuzzled against my ass. With my fingers in Robin's ass, I began to pull him towards me and pull his ass to my cock.

The circle began to contract, as each man's cock got closer to his neighbor's quivering hole. I shivered again as Ronnie's organ pushed against my hole. My ass wasn't lubricated, but Ronnie must have been oozing enough to slip in without discomfort. Sean was moaning as Ram fucked him.

Ronnie eased his knob into my ass, but once it was in, he thrust the rest into the depths of my body. As he did, I rammed Robin. Robin's ass was needy. He needed another man's cock in his ass to be complete. He cried in pleasure as he fucked Jack while I massaged his ass. Soon we were all connected.

"Stroke! Stroke! Stroke!" the Earl called out. Soon cocks plunged into asses in a rhythmic pattern. Ram was the first man to shoot his seed. The first ejaculation started a chain reaction of orgasms. Each man drained his balls into his mate's ass as another man filled his ass with man seed.

Ronnie had been disciplined as he obeyed the Earl's commands, but once he began to climax, he became a wild man. He grabbed my shoulders to insure I took every inch of his rod. I felt him twitch as each squirt of man seed was projected from his organ. It was lovely.

The party was over now. We were spent. I returned to my college with the Earl and his retinue. The next week was quiet and I was much involved with my studies. There were many students who didn't seem to study at all, but I was cursed with my father's intellectual curiosity. I enjoyed getting beneath the surface of academics. Several weeks later Ronnie appeared at the gate and asked to speak with me.

"Sir Edmund wanted to know if you might attend him later this afternoon?" he asked. "He will be at his offices."

"I should be able to do that," I said. "Is this some special occasion?"

Ronnie smiled. "Not at all. He was away in London arranging for expeditions for the last two weeks," Ronnie replied. "I think he just wants to renew your acquaintance. Is 5:00 acceptable for you?" I said yes.

Sir Edmund's office was in the Oxford Museum, a modern building of unusual design that enclosed a cast iron and glass display area. Skeletons, fossilized dinosaurs and curiosities filled the light and airy room. I asked for Sir Edmund and a porter took me to the top floor of the building and then into the attic. His office was in the turret roof over the main entrance. It was a gigantic space, filled with large drawings, specimens in glass jars and a green house area filled with exotic plants.

"Mr. Fairbairn, it's so good to see you again," Sir Edmund said. "Welcome to the mad scientist's lair!"

"I had no idea such a space existed," I said. "It's good to see you again." We shook hands. Ronnie went to the door and closed it behind him. Professor Woolrich emerged from a dark corner of the room and greeted me warmly.

"You know I am not one to beat around the bush," Sir Edmund said. "I enjoyed meeting you two weeks ago. I was hoping you took it well. I was afraid it might have been too much for a man of your character and upbringing."

"I assure you I enjoyed it as much as you, if not more so," I said. "I have to admit until earlier this year I was a novice in matters sexual."

"Your introduction was gentle?" Isaac asked.

"At first it was gentle, but when things became more intense and forceful I was so excited, it made no impact on my emotions," I said. "To tell you the truth, at first, I was unsure I could participate, but my natural urges took over. At least I hope they were natural urges. There seems to be a drive that takes control of my actions."

"Indeed there is," Sir Edmund exclaimed. "I once thought myself too refined and cultured to be driven by sexual urges. This is pure, unadulterated foolishness. Isaac and I have found a circle of friends who share our enthusiasm. We were hoping you would like to join us."

"I do," I said.

"Most of our friends are older men," Isaac added. "You may have noted, they are quite varied in social status. That doesn't bother you?"

"Not at all," I said. "The Earl and Ram must have told you about my earlier experiences."

"They did," Sir Edmund replied. "I thought you might be a like spirit. Let me be direct. We would like you to join our group. Frankly, we would like to have a man who could satisfy the desires of some for relations with a younger man. I seemed to me you liked relations with them, so it is good for all."

"It seemed to me you had several younger men at the gathering."

"Sean and Billy were good men, but they are humble men. There is a chance they are simply submitting to men of higher rank," Isaac said.

"Lord Cloverton?"

Edmund laughed. "He certainly is willing, that is clear! I like Robin, but his interest are well beyond what can be regarded as normal. He is usually entirely passive. You are..."

"Both passive and active and well-hung!" Isaac added. We all laughed.

"I am honored," I said as I bowed to the men in mock seriousness. "Do you have regular... meetings?"

"We would like to, but it is never as regular as we might wish. Most of us are men of affairs and scheduling is difficult," Edmund said. "We do have a token to identify members." He removed a small box from his pocket. In it was a gold signet ring. It was simple and small and embellished only with an engraved image of a cock, a rooster, not the male organ. He slipped it on my finger.

"You are now a member of the Rising at Dawn Society," Edmund said. "We meet twice a year for a breakfast at dawn. Informal meetings occur when members encounter each other. Saturday afternoon there will be a gathering at Isaac's house. Can you attend?" I nodded. We shook hands and I returned to my college.

A day later, I got an invitation to Isaac's house for tea at 3:00. It was a pretty day and I walked to his cottage. While it was quite near Oxford the house was quite secluded and I might not have found it if I hadn't encountered another member of the Society who knew the way.

"Are you lost?" he asked.

"I'm not lost yet, but I may be soon," I replied. I saw his ring and moved my hand so he could see mine.

He smiled. "Follow me!" he said. "Isaac's taste in gardening tends to favor the over grown. I'm Seth Lamb."

"I'm Robert Fairbairn," I replied. Seth was a big man who dressed in expensive, but rather loud clothes. "Are you related to the inventor?"

"My father is an inventive man," I said. "He has a knack for inventing machinery."

"I'm deeply honored to make your acquaintance," Seth replied. "I've worked on doing the same sort of thing, and I was shocked when I found he had already created what I had been working on for years. It is a most impressive achievement." We had reached a big hedge. Going through a small maze, we arrived at Isaac's cottage. This was indeed an ancient, half-timbered house. While it was ancient, it was in good condition. Isaac greeted us and we went in the place. It was a warm and sunny autumn day and the house was comfortable.

To the rear was a small garden surrounded by a great hedge, making the place entirely cut off from the outside world. Standing in the garden were Ram, Big Jack, Earnest and much to my surprise, Ralph, the Smithy. All of them were naked.

"Leave your clothes in the house," Isaac said. "I will join you when the last guest arrives." I had never been naked outside, but, as always, I did as I was told. Seth was portly. However, he had been muscular and he was still solid. His belly was impressive, but the family jewels hung low and very visible below the paunch. A big bulge in the foreskin gave promise of an impressive organ. He went to Ram and Big Jack and I went to Ralph. Earnest looked uneasy but Ralph put his arm around his shoulders. Earnest relaxed as he felt Ralph's protective embrace.

"Do you know these folks?" Ralph asked. "Ram said I'd like them."

"Very much so, I think," I answered. I glance at Seth who was already on his knees sucking Big Jack and Ram.

Ralph smiled. "Everyone is really shy, I see," he remarked. He dropped to his knees and sucked me. Earnest smiled and joined Ralph at my cock. I got Ralph to stand so I could suck him. Sir Edmund arrived with Ronnie and two other men, I didn't know. Edmund joined Seth, Big Jack and Ram. The other men joined us.

"Is there room for more?" one man asked.

"Of course," Ralph said as he rose. The sun showed off every hair on his body and I saw him as an ancient god, like Odin, or Thor. "Ralph's the name," He said to the new man.

"I'm Lord..." the man started to say. "Frederick Karl is my name." He had a slight German accent. He was a slim and trim body with a coat of blond hair on his chest. Frederick Karl wasn't handsome so much as he was elegant and almost delicate. The contrast between him and the massive blacksmith was striking.

Frederick Karl put his hand out and stroked Ralph's reddish pelt in clear admiration. "Wotan," he said as he sank to his knees and tried to swallow Ralph's cock in a single gulp.

The man with Frederick was short and stocky. With a barrel chest and massive shoulders, he was an impressive specimen of manhood. "I am Max," he said in a very strong German accent.

"I am Robert. This is Earnest," I said. "Earnest is deaf, so he may have a hard time understanding." Max didn't understand that, but after some gestures, he figured it out.

"My brother is deaf," Max, said in German. Max went over to Earnest and hugged him. All was well. Isaac came with a final guest, a white bearded Indian, who was naked except for a turban. He must have been sixty but was in good condition and he must have been well over six feet tall.

The Indian looked at the assembled men, saw me and came to me like an iron filing to a magnet. Isaac came with him. "Robert, this is Ravi. His English isn't as good as Ram's. But he'd like to meet you," Isaac said.

Ravi's skin was dark and his chest was covered in black hair that was beginning to turn white. He was uncertain what to do, but his cock was rock hard and sticking straight out. The sunlight glistened on a bead of precum that appeared on his slit. I collected it on my finger and then licked it. Ravi smiled.

CHAPTER 6

Meeting new people is hard for me. I am naturally shy and reserved. Oddly, it was easier for me to meet men who are naked. I think the sexual excitement generated by the naked man overcomes my natural reticence. Nudity removed barriers. Ravi was partly erect when he met me. As soon as we chatted for a minute, he was fully erect and oozing cock juices. There was no way for him to hide his feelings.

My cock responded the same way. He knew I was excited and willing. Ravi liked that. We embraced. I felt him shiver when our cocks touched. As had happened before, I was pleased Ravi responded to me. I was 20 and I sometimes thought of myself as a boy. I had never thought of myself as an object of desire.

I had seen steel engravings of the sack of Rome by the barbarians and of an orgy at the palace of Caligula. In each, the youths cowered and fear. This gathering in the garden of Isaac's house must have met the definition of an orgy, but that wasn't the way it felt. I felt a sense of brotherhood with these men, not fear. I knew they wanted to have sex with me and bury their members deep in my ass. I wanted the same. We would be sharing and mingling our body's juices and our man seed. We would pool our resources to achieve mutual pleasure. It would have been a fantasy come true, if my fantasies were much more exciting than they actually were.

I had also come to recognize the difference between naked and nude. I had noticed this with Ralph when I first saw him washing up in the yard. I previously had seen being undressed as an embarrassment. It was a fleeting moment between taking off one set of clothes off and putting on another. Ralph was unashamed of his body. He was comfortable and at ease.

I think Earnest and I were the only ones who were at all uneasy here and that unease vanished as we came to know the guests. The men were unashamed of their bodies and of their desires. Each man had his own interests, but each was willing to accommodate the other men's urges.

As I pondered these things, I looked at the other men. Frederick Karl was standing as Ralph sucked his cock. Karl was beautiful and elegant. Ralph was well equipped to play the role of a Viking raider. Frederick Karl shivered a little and changed to a wider stance. I saw Ralph had a finger in Karl's hole and Karl moved to permit deeper penetration.

Max was clearly interested in Earnest. He was on his knees worshiping the deaf man's cock. Max looked as if he was suckling at his mother's breast. Earnest had his eyes closed as he enjoyed the sensations.

I returned to my embrace with Ravi. Ram came over to us with a bottle of oil. He got behind me, oiled his finger and knelt at my rear as he began to lubricate my ass. I knew he was preparing me for Ravi. He used one finger, then two and three as he opened my hole. With his other hand, he coated Ravi's meat. It looked like a rod of black steel.

Ravi pulled back his foreskin exposing his head. The cock head was almost iridescent, pink and lavender. His seed slit almost bisected the tender, but bloated gland. He was so hard it looked as if it hurt, but I knew that wasn't what he was feeling.

Ram pulled me to the ground on top of him. He was a human cushion. He grabbed my legs and pulled them up and spreading them wide to expose my hole for Ravi. Ravi got on his knees and rested his oiled cock at my hole. I was at the perfect height for him.

Ravi was both gentle and forceful. He took his time working the head into my ass, then made several strong thrusts to be fully embedded. He had no single technique that would drive single-mindedly toward the orgasm; rather he had a repertoire of varied actions. He switched from one to another. As soon as I was accustomed to gentle pluses, he changed to deep thrusts. When I got use to these, he pulled his cock back so only his head was in rubbing my nut.

After a while, I gave up trying to anticipate his next movement. I relaxed and let the sensations flow over me, like waves at the ocean. He smiled at me when I relaxed. This was what he wanted. His cock was a faucet that filled pleasure into my receptive body. I could do nothing but feel pleasure.

He pulled me forward off Ram's body and on to his. Now I was sitting on his cock. I am not a small man, and he couldn't move his hips. I rotated mine and soon was doing a primitive dance on his pole. I wanted to make sure his cock touched every part of my ass. This dance got wild until he began to twitch and shiver. I felt the blast of his man seed into my ass.

I cried out as I felt my seed build up until I couldn't hold back. Max appeared out of nowhere. He fed Ravi his cock and bent over to take my cock into his mouth just in time to take my first volley. It was lovely. When I finished ejaculating, I rolled off Ravi's body.

Isaac was there and he held my legs open so he could lick my ass. My sphincter was stretched and felt sore. I wouldn't say it had been abused, but it certainly had been well used. At first, I thought he wanted to caress the sore opening, but that wasn't his only objective. He wanted to open my hole and coax Ravi's man seed from my ass. This shocked me, but oddly I seemed to have involuntarily relaxed my opening and some of the man juices drooled out.

Seth, the rather portly businessman came over. "Let me help you with that," he said to Isaac. Isaac got out of the way and Seth slipped his short, but very thick cock into my ass. He gently thrust it in a few times, and then pulled out. Isaac went after Seth's cum covered cock with gusto. Isaac licked my ass hole again, and then Seth went in for a second time. I was exhausted and all but fell asleep.

Apparently, most of the men had climaxed and there was a lull in the activity. It was a beautiful and warm day. We were on the grass. Some were resting, others chatted quietly. Ralph came over to me and sat. He wore the cock signet ring, like me.

"The Maharajah enjoyed you," he said.

"Ravi's a... ?" I blurted out.

Ralph nodded. "He was a close friend of Ram's father. He thought Ram had been killed by his brothers. It was a great surprise when he discovered him with the Earl," Ralph said. "Apparently Ravi and Ram's father were lovers."

"He seems like a good man," I said.

"Ravi believes sex and orgasms are man's connection to god. He's Hindu, so I'm not sure which god, but it connects you to some god," Ralph explained.

"As a Maharajah he can take anyone he wants," I remarked.

"That's not the way he sees it," Ralph continued. "He believes sex must be pure. If you do it for personal gain or advancement, it's defiled. If you do it because it's your duty, it's defiled."

"When is it acceptable?"

"It's acceptable when it done purely for pleasure," Ralph said. "He visits here every three or four years. Here sex is pure. Let's swim."

"Swim?"

"Yes, there's an old Mill pond on the other side of the garden," he said. I followed him through a brake in the hedge and followed a grassy path to the pond. It was beautiful and the water was refreshing.

Sir Edmund, Ronnie and Frederick Karl joined us. The water was like the sherbet course in a grand dinner. It cleansed the palate so we could enjoy the next course. Eventually everyone came to the pool and took a swim. Isaac had a hammock between two trees. Frederic Karl got in it. It had two straps I hadn't noticed. Isaac tied the straps to his legs. Like the rest of his body, Frederick Karl had a beautiful ass. I was a sweet little rose bud.

"Our fried Frederick Karl has volunteered to be our mid day entertainment," Sir Edmund said as he squirted some lubricant in the man's ass.

We gathered around him and took our turns fucking. Earnest was the first to pop his cock into the waiting ass. The second Earnest's knob was on the dark side of the ass; Frederick Karl got a blissful look on his face. Earnest looked slightly bewildered. He was a boiler stoker who was fucking a beautiful noble man and the noble clearly loved it. Like Lord Cloverton, Frederick Karl needed a cock in his body to be complete.

After a few minutes, Earnest exclaimed, "I'm going to shoot." He started to pull out, but Frederick Karl ordered, "Fill me up!" It was a command, not a request, but Earnest was more than willing to comply. Earnest's entire body convulsed with each ejaculation. He rammed his partner hard as he shot. When he pulled out, Big Jack took his place. Earnest had been gentle. He made love to Frederick Karl. Big Jack was a man rammer. He reminded me of one of my Father's machines, going at full speed.

In spite of the aggressive pounding of Frederick Karl, Big Jack didn't shoot off quickly. I was worried the man in the hammock couldn't take it, but I worried in vain. Karl maintained a blissful look and an impressive erection throughout the session. Finally, Big Jack stood still, almost frozen. The only movement was in his ass, which quivered as he pumped his seed. He pulled out and Ram replaced him.

I was to the side so I could see his hole and the little rosebud. The rose bud vanished in a split second when Big Jack rammed him. When Ram's monster head touched it, he hesitated and just rested the organ at the opening. Frederick Karl opened his ass in invitation. Ram pushed the head in part way and stopped. The ass muscles quivered and opened again, trying to entice the gland into the dark recesses. Ram pushed in part way several more times, but never beyond the flared edge of his cock head. Poor Frederick Karl's ass had nothing to grip.

Finally, Ram miscalculated and the entire head vanished into the ass. I saw the ass tighten as Karl grabbed it. Frederick Karl almost passed out in pleasure.

Cocks are as varied in size and shape as are men, but Frederick Karl showed no favoritism. He liked them all. He didn't get tired and he didn't lose his enthusiasm. I was sixth in line. I thought this was going to be a mechanical procedure, but that wasn't the case. His ass was filled with cream and I expected to slip in easily. His ass lips were still firm and I had to push to break into the inner sanctum. He twitched as my knob rubbed his prostate. Frederick Karl shivered in sexual excitement. As I churned the man seed soup in his ass, I felt the same excitement.

After playing with his delicate pink tits, I bent over to kiss him. As I did, Isaac worked his well-lubricated member into my hole. This caught me by surprise, but it was a pleasant surprise. I was a bit disoriented at first, but soon the three of us developed an easy rhythm. When Isaac was fully embedded, I felt as if his cock was touching mine and we formed a single organ.

Isaac pulled out suddenly and a larger cock rammed me. It was Ralph. I couldn't hold back any longer. My seed joined the soup in Karl's rectum. As my body twitched with each ejaculation Ralph said, "Damn, that's good."

When I pulled out, Ralph took my place in Frederick's ass. It took only one or two thrusts to dump his balls' contents into Frederick Karl. Isaac was last in line. We got Frederick Karl out of the hammock and we went back into the pool.

"That was nice," Sir Edmund said to Ralph. "It's been a while since we did that." Ralph nodded.

"Is that a normal part of your get together?" I asked.

"Heavens no," Edmund said. "We only do it for Frederick Karl when he can get here. He was once the Crown Prince's favorite playmate until Bismarck discovered the attachment. He was sent into exile to live here with some of his English relatives. Alas, none of them could appreciate his skills, except for... I won't go into that," Edmund remarked. "He was a very unhappy man when I met him."

"Who introduced you?" I asked.

"No one," Edmund said, "He came to Oxford and became one of my students. He is a gifted and intelligent man. That would not be appreciated in the Crown Prince's circle, but I did appreciate it." Sir Edmund leaned close to me and whispered. "He was afraid of sexual relations with a person not of his rank. That is most limiting to a man of his elevated status. I'm afraid I made a democrat of him, indeed a liberal democrat."

I smiled. "He seems to have overcome that hurdle!"

Edmund nodded. "When he first met your friend Ralph, Frederick Karl climaxed hands free the second Ralph's knob touched Karl's hole," he explained. CIt was beautiful."

"Ralph almost did the same to me," I said.

When we got out of the water, Ronnie set out tea. I again thought about the engraving of Caligula's orgy. I wondered if he served tea. I laughed aloud.

"And what is the reason for your merriment?" Seth asked. I told him of my visions. Everyone was amused. Sir Edmund thought it was hilarious.

"You do realize that Oxford is one of the few places in the world where you will find people who know what Caligula served," he said. "I suspect there are a number of men who would like to have been there in person." There was more laughter.

"I always serve tea," Ravi said. "That and a little potion."

"What kind of a potion?" Max asked. He was sitting next to Earnest, fondling the stoker's genitals.

"It is very fast acting, and of short duration, but during the time it works, it renders you insatiable," Ravi said. "My father used it on my mother when I was conceived. Ram's father always claimed it had become a part of me. My appetites are hard to satisfy."

"Do you think Caligula took the potion?" Isaac asked.

"I rather doubt it," Ravi explained. "It tends to make you want to give and take pleasure in equal amounts. I should not have mentioned it, since I don't have any with me. Perhaps the next time I visit I will bring some with me. The sun was beginning to set and it was getting cold. We returned to the house, got dressed and left.

Sir Edmund and Isaac left on expedition after the party, and life quieted down. I became much involved in my studies. Much to my surprise, my father's scientific interests became more pronounced in me. I found hydraulics to be fascinating. That could hardly be a less stylish course of study possible at Oxford at that time. I continued to see Tristan and Ovid, but we grew apart. Their interests and mine diverged.

I was surprised when one of my professors submitted one of my papers to a scientific organization, and it was accepted for presentation at the annual meeting in London. I wrote my father and told him of the honor. He arranged to attend the Royal Association of Engineers meeting as a guest. My paper related to calculating the speed and pressure of water passing through constricted spaces, i.e. pipes. I thought the subject was dry and technical, but the Royal Association received it warmly. When they accepted the paper, they hadn't realized I was Sir Robert Fairbairn's son. My father was much admired

I was surprised to see Frederick Karl and Max in the audience. They came to me afterward and I introduced them to my Father. They invited us to visit them while we were in London. My father had to return to his work the next morning, so they asked me to lunch after I took my father to the train station.

Frederick Karl lived in an elegant house in Belgravia. It was furnished in the most modern style and I almost expected to find William Morris himself there. Indeed, the house was decorated by Mr. Morris. It was very elegant indeed. It was a small luncheon, but the other guests included his sister and her husband, and several friends from Oxford. It was presented as the guest of honor and much to my surprise; no one seemed to think my scientific interests were anything other than admirable.

He provided a carriage to take me back to my hotel. The driver was a man named Cecil. When he opened the door for me, I saw he had a cock signet ring. I made sure he noticed mine. He winked at me. "Are you in a rush sir?" he asked.

"I am free for the rest of the day," I replied.

"I was going to pay a visit to a friend in Chelsea," Cecil said. "Would you like to join me?"

"Would your friend enjoy meeting me?"

Clive smiled. "I wouldn't worry about that at all. He's a good man."

I agreed and we traveled across the city to Chelsea. It was a long trip. London is a large city and I came to appreciate its vastness. We stopped at a new house and Clive rang the bell. "Mr. Sargent please," he said. The servant let us in the house. It was richly decorated and filled with paintings. I looked at the beautiful works. All were painted by John Singer Sargent. We were in his house.

A handsome, bearded man came to greet us. "Clive, you brought a friend," Mr. Sargent said. He was obviously pleased to see me.

"This is Robert Fairbairn. He an Oxford man," Clive said. "He's in town presenting a paper to the Royal Association of Engineers."

Mr. Sargent looked me over and saw the cock signet. He moved his hand and showed me his ring. "Pleased to meet a man who has reached such heights at a tender age. You are to be congratulated," he said. "Let's go to my studio where we can chat." We followed him to the attic of the house where we found a huge, brilliantly lighted studio.

There were three men in the studio. One was his servant, Nicola, and a Negro man named Pierre. They were nude and had evidently been modeling for the artist. The third man was an ample gentleman with an extravagant beard. He was apparently an artist as he was sketching the two men.

"Freddy this is a budding young man of science Robert Fairbairn. You know Cedric Mills, I believe." Sargent said in introduction. Freddy smiled and nodded toward Cecil. "Robert this is Sir Frederic Leighton." He was a well-known artist.

We politely exchanged greetings. Sir Frederic wore the ring too. All was as conventional as it could be except for the two nude models. "Is this all of our guests?" Sargent asked.

"As far as I know," Cecil replied. "Frederick Karl is occupied for the afternoon." He began to undress.

Sargent wore a brocaded coat in scarlet and gold. It looked like the robe of a Renaissance Prince. He opened it with a flourish and threw it on a chair. He was nude too. Leighton was wearing an artist's smock. When he removed that, he was nude. The models had been standing perfectly still until Leighton disrobed. He sketched through the introductions.

They now joined us. Curiously their genitals were perfectly relaxed when the posed. When they stood to join us, they were firming up. A short while later they were erect. Everyone was hard except for me. I was a bit nervous. Sargent immediately bent over to solve that problem. He swallowed my entire cock, and then sucked it until I was fully engaged. I thought he would pull back when I was erect, since I'm big and it's hard to take it all. He had no problem at all.

Pierre came over to us and shoved his cock into Sargent's ass. Sargent shivered when that happened, but immediately resumed sucking me with greater gusto. Cecil was sucking Leighton. Nicola came over to me. "Just stay still. I'm going to lubricate your hole," he said in a strong Italian accent. It was going to be a good afternoon.

CHAPTER 7

John Singer Sargent was an elegant looking man and most distinguished. He was thin, tall and had a carefully groomed beard. His mannerisms were slightly effete and elegant too. His chest was dusted with hair and his genitals were elegant too. They were Greek statue like, although they were more generously scaled. He had the equipment of a man, not a boy.

Nicola, the model, was shaved smooth except for the bush. He was thin and his muscles were well defined. I guessed he was a perfect model. His skin was olive toned, but he was handsome. His cock was definitely on the large side of average.

Sir Frederic was a bear of a man. He had an extravagant beard and a fur covered chest. He was heavy set, but not what you would consider fat. Obviously, he ate well. Frederic's cock was fat and long. His balls were goat or bull like. I would say he would be a good prototype for Zeus, mature, but still fertile and manly.

Pierre was a black Hercules. His musculature was magnificent and impressive. He too was shaved smooth except for a well-groomed patch at his cock. His heavy balls hung low. The sack seemed almost transparent, so you could see each apricot sized testicle in detail. His cock was perhaps eight or nine inches long and his knob was large and well defined.

The final member of our group, Cedric, looked dumpy in his coachman's dress. He wasn't the elegant man in livery, but rather the man who wore heavy clothes well suited for a man who worked with horses. Naked he was a good manly specimen. He was quite muscular and well formed. His hair was the color of burnished copper and was continuous from his well-cropped beard to his toes. It was a thick coat, but since it was red, it didn't hide the body below. He had creamy skin, with pink nipples and pink cock head. When he was erect, there was a blue tone to the head.

When I look at a man, I tend to fantasize a personality that matches the appearance. With two well-known and distinguished artists, two artist models and a coachman, I had a vision of each man's personality. I was wrong about all of my suppositions.

I had forgotten that social status and station vanish when one is naked. Older and more ancient signs of status become dominant. Sargent and Leighton became our equals and the lone black man with his huge organ became the master. That was the fantasy, but not the reality. The black man, Pierre, was an artist from Senegal who had been educated in Paris. He spoke French beautifully and English well.

I later found out Pierre loved Sargent and he wanted to maintain his "connection intimate" with his lover. In his thinking, once he was lodged in the artist's ass, they formed single sexual unit. Pierre got excited as Sargent sucked me. He shared the experience.

Nicola had no such complicated vision. His cock was well shaped and it slid into my ass effortlessly. At first, it was just mildly pleasurable, but as he slowly massaged my rectum, the pleasure built.

We were all in an ungainly position. After a minute or two, we broke apart and reformed ourselves to a large ottoman or divan on the side of the room.

"Robert, I'd like to tell you my interest," Sargent said as we relocated. "I love passion and my objective is to postpone the orgasmic moment as long as possible. I love to teeter on the edge of the climax. My hope is to turn those exquisite moments of sexual ecstasy into minutes and even hours."

"It seems to me that this is much like playing with a pistol that is cocked and ready," I said.

Sargent smiled. "I didn't say I always achieve my objective. Sometimes you miscalculate, sometimes one gets carried away," he said. "At one time I loved multiple orgasms, but my age has betrayed me. You are young; I assume you have no problem climaxing several times."

"That has happened," I said.

He smiled. We sat on the pillow-covered divan. I got on the bed and sucked Sargent's member as he sucked mine. Pierre walked up to us, raised Sargent's leg and pushed his shiny black knob into the quivering ass. It was easy and almost casual as if sexual penetration was an every day event. I saw Sargent's ass quiver a moment in anticipation of the entry. As the cock pushed deeper into the artist's ass, Sargent rewarded me with a burst of precum.

Pierre's cock was well oiled and it had the aspect of a steel or iron rod. It looked so hard I thought it might hurt. The artist's oozing cock told me that was foolishness. I could easily take Sargent's entire member into my mouth. This meant I was only three inches from Pierre's cock. As I watched the huge member slowly pump, I found myself getting even more excited. Pierre would pull all the way out and then toy with the eager hole. As he did this, I sensed Sargent getting tense, waiting for the pleasure of the next entry.

Once Pierre stroked his cock and coaxed a blob of his cock juices out of the wide slit. I stuck out my tongue and tasted it. Another time he picked up the pace. He pulled out and shot a single ribbon of man seed into my mouth. I immediately returned to sucking Sargent's cock and bathed it in Pierre's seed. I thought he would shoot the remainder into the artist's hole, but he save it for later.

Pierre was one of those rare men who had total control of his ejaculations. He had the will power to hold back and stop an orgasm, and then unload it later. Usually that was in Sargent's mouth or ass.

I assumed Nicola would return to my hole, but Cecil had taken his place. Over the next half hour, Cecil, Nicola and Frederic took their turns at my ass. They weren't at all interested in Sargent's delayed orgasm scheme. This was good, since they seemed to have graded their cocks by size. The man with the smallest cock fucked me first, followed by the man with a bigger cock. Each man shot his cream into me. The mixture of Cecil's Anglo Saxon cream with Nicola's Italian seed was just right to ease the entrance of Frederic's more challenging organ.

Sir Frederic's cock hurt some at first. I got use to it and soon I felt it was worth it. Frederic was very much a fucker not a lover. Fortunately, he had a good sense of what my ass and I could take. It would be safe to say he was always one-step ahead of me. It wasn't as pleasant as Cecil or Nicola, but it was more purely sexual. While it was good for me, it was better for Sargent. He loved watching Frederic pounding me like a crazed madman. From his vantage point sucking my member, he saw it and tasted my reaction. His hold back the orgasm scheme collapsed when he flooded my mouth with his man seed.

Frederic's orgasm followed as he watched his friend fill my mouth. This may seem odd. However, I felt intense pleasure as the seed receptacle for these two gifted men. I thought how wonderful it would have been to live in Italy during the Renaissance. I would have been perfectly happy to drain Michelangelo's manly seed.

When Sargent got off the divan, Cecil replaced him. His cock was shorter but tasty. After Sargent's salty seed, Cecil produced rich and sweet cock honey. I was enjoying this elixir when a large object poked at my ass. It was Pierre.

A half hour earlier when I entered the studio, I would never have considered taking the huge organ, what a difference a half hour can make. If Sir Frederic had been a somewhat crude fucking machine, Pierre was an artist well skilled in the anal arts. Given the size of his member, he was both considerate and delicate.

Cecil, Nicola and Frederic had already deposited their cream in my rear. My ass was certainly well prepared. It would be crude to say Pierre fucked me. He politely knocked at the door. I opened it and let him in. It was odd in that while he was both polite and almost gentile, he was also relentless. Every time I could focus, the huge object was deeper in my ass. As with Frederic, he played with my hole and sphincter. Only when the sphincter lost any ability to resist did he push deeper. By that time, I disparately wanted it.

I was both excited and relaxed. I hadn't believed that combination was possible. I knew full penetration was inevitable, but every movement of the black rod filled me with indescribably intense pleasure.

Cecil wasn't sucking on my cock; he was just licking up what drooled from my organ. I was like a baby sucking at his mother's breast. Cecil's cock honey flowed continuously. Whenever the flow seemed to abate, I would try to suction more from his balls. His balls were well shaped, but I marveled they could be so productive.

At some point, I seemed to have lost myself. I became a sexual appendage to Cecil and Pierre. I was feeling only pleasure and giving only pleasure. Even today, I pity the person who hasn't experienced the feeling of total sexual involvement.

Pierre lost control and he flooded me with his seed. I could feel him squirting in my ass. I shot off and Cecil was nice enough to lick it all up. We broke apart and rested on the divan. I was so exhausted I could hardly move.

I was surprised when Sargent came over to me and fingered my well-stretched hole. He got on his knees, lifted my legs and licked the tender opening. Frederic came over to feed me is cock. It was soft now but still a mouthful. I got my tongue into the foreskin and licked the underside of the glans. He shivered a little when I did this, so I continued.

"Mr. Fairbairn, you are a marvel," he said. "I don't recall another novice who has taken to our merry band as well as you. You are a master of the erotic arts." He played with my nipples, but got no reaction. "One of my more clever friends claimed I had a brain in my cock. He thought I was a libertine and exhausted my talents in sexual experimentation. I have come to believe he was right. Not about the wasted talents mind you, but about the brain. In some ways that little brain in the cock takes us back to our origins."

"In my own case, Sir Frederic, I'm afraid the brain in my cock may well be bigger than that in my head," Cecil interjected. There was general laughter.

"Without that little brain we might become mere logical machines," Sir Frederic continued. "In this modern age we are so tempted to let logic and science takes charge of our lives. I agree and indeed admire science, but the most impressive scientist can easily fall to the demands of the cock. Logic flies out the window when sex rears its attractive head."

"I do not believe the cock has a brain," Pierre stated in his strong French accent. "I believe it is the great sensory organ. The intensity of feeling in a cock dwarfs the eye, nose, tongue or ears in its power. Mr. Fairbairn is a handsome man, if not a beautiful one. When he opened his body to me and let me probe his deepest recess, I realized he might well be a great man. I felt that with my cock, not with my eyes or ears."

We chatted between fondling, and sucking cocks. Everyone was partially, or fully erect. I think anyone listening to the conversation would think this was just a risqué talk between academics. It was hard to believe the atmosphere was so relaxed and casual, while the sexual activity was so intense.

Unfortunately, I was expected to be at dinner with several friends, so I had to leave at five. Cecil took me to my hotel. He told me I had been a great success with the men and with him personally. "It's unusual for Pierre to screw anyone but John," Cecil said. "I thought his seed was for John's use only. You must have inspired him."

"I'll take that as compliment," I said.

"Mr. Sargent has many acquaintances, but many aren't willing to sport with a man in my station," Cecil continued. "Sure, they'll fuck me, but I love the warmth of a man's backside."

I smiled. "I surely enjoyed your visit," I said.

"If we meet again, I'd love to sample you cream," he said. We were at my hotel so we parted. One would think that having been in a wild sexual orgy and being fucked by several men might leave a mark on you, but no one in the lobby noticed a thing. I bathed, dressed and when to the Explorer's Club where several of my Professors and friends had a most elaborate dinner arranged.

These were not my older friends, such as Tristan and Ovid. They were colleagues in my scientific studies. I must confess my attraction to Tristan and Ovid had greatly diminished.

I had break between sessions, and was on my own. My life was taking a turn toward the academic and scientific. They were preparing to be gentlemen of leisure. My Father had taken a steamer for New York where he was planning to build a factory. He suggested that I travel.

While my plan was to visit Paris and then Rome, I began the trip with a short jaunt to visit Ralph. I sent him a letter saying I would be passing through. He replied by asking me to stay with him. He did note he would have some visitors on Sunday, but he thought I would like them.

I got to his cottage on Wednesday. He was hard at work, so I took a pleasant walk around the countryside. The weather was unusually beautiful and I enjoyed myself immensely. I returned to the cottage in time to watch him wash up, naked in the yard. When I first saw him, I had been a virgin, now I was experienced. I wondered if the excitement I had felt earlier would vanish. It didn't. If anything, I was more excited.

We had a simple dinner and sat down to checkers. As before, Ralph beat me regularly although I did manage to eke out two wins. I told him about my trip to London and my paper. He seemed excited for me. While I had been uneasy when he beat me at checkers when we first met, I realized he had genuine pleasure at my success.

I had dreamed of meeting Ralph again and returning to the bed where I had first coupled with him. I was shocked when Ralph told me he had the same dream.

"I dreamed we were stranded on an island as in Robinson Caruso. We were starving and the only food was your seed. I would suck the seed from your balls and then you'd beg me to do it again. Somehow your cream got thicker and more plentiful as I sucked you over and over again," he said.

"Did I get nothing to eat?" I asked.

He smiled. "Indeed you did, but you insisted I deliver my ball juices into your arse. You said there was less loss to evaporation that way. I thought that might not be true, but you're a learned gentleman and you must have known."

"I can see myself saying that just to feel you member in my ass," I said. "Did your dream have a happy ending?"

"It didn't end. It just continued like a perpetual motion machine," he explained. "I'd suck up your seed then shoot the same amount into you. It was a bit like the loaves and fishes, or perhaps manna from heaven."

"What do you mean?"

"At first you shot a normal load, but then it double and tripled. My mouth was filled and I had to swallow," he explained.

I laughed. "If that was the manna in Exodus, I think the Israelites would have had a happy forty years in the wilderness!"

It was late and we went to bed to see if we could recreate Ralph's dream. We only were able to recreate half of his dream. Once he was in my ass, I was loath to let him go. Ralph did his part and fucked me all night long.

I awoke with an understanding of why primitive peoples thought sexual experienced were mystical experiences. Compared to the run of the mill of daily experiences and events, sex was of an entirely different level.

I had been afraid my first coupling with Ralph was a onetime only event. Perhaps the series of sexual encounters since that meeting would make that first time seem more ordinary and pedestrian. In reality, I felt the opposite. My enjoyment of Ralph's person and his cock was enhanced. The shock of his first penetration was past. Now I could savor the connection. His cock head would toy with my sphincter until I was desperate for that moment when he popped through the sphincter's barrier and slip deep into my body.

Ralph knew when he hit my prostate. He would linger there and massage the tender gland with his cock head. I learned how to undulate my hips to give him more pleasure. Now I could sense his tension increase as he approached the orgasmic moment. He was the most gentle of lovers until that moment. A second or two before he climaxed, he would all but pull out of me and then ram me hard. All was well with the world.

CHAPTER 8

My father gave me a trip to Paris as a Christmas present. I had never been outside Britain and I jumped at the chance. Paris was wonderful. With little industry, it seemed modern, clean and elegant compared to the somber streets of London. I went to see all the sites of interest. There was little trace of the disastrous war with Prussia. The Opera had been finished, and there was no trace of the burned out hulk of the Napoleon III's palace, the Tuilleries. All was new, bright and modern. The city seemed to be in a perpetual state of carnival.

As I expected, artists of the most advanced sort seemed to be everywhere. I am not art critic, but I found many modern paintings attractive. They were light and sun filled. I actually bought several from a gifted man named Manet.

I also found some like spirits in the French engineering community. I met two men, Edgar LaVille, and Pierre Montjoi who shared my interests in hydraulics. They spoke English as badly as I spoke French. We got along well. They showed me all the technical high points of the city.

I also discovered we shared an interest in things other than technology. I knew they were friends. I hadn't realized how truly close they were. Edgar was 45 or 50 and had been a military engineer in the French army. Pierre was the son of one of his fellow officer. Pierre's father was killed at the battle of Sedan, and Edgar took him under his wing.

We were a most congenial trio. My French got better as they improved their English. While they were most interested in things technical, they also were interested in art, music and archeology. They introduced me to fine food and good wine. After a night of too much good wine, we all shared a bed. I woke and found Pierre nursing on Edgar's cock. I joined in. It seemed as if it were the most natural thing in the world.

We were perfectly sexually compatible too. Pierre was a slim and masculine man of 27. He had a hairy chest and a cock that was both thin and very long. Edgar was a bull of a man with a thick and massive member. His cock was as thick as Pierre's was long. My long and moderately thick cock was a great success with them

Our first night together was oral. On the next night, we progressed successfully into anal intercourse. It was good, but when Pierre and I discovered Edgar could take both of our cocks. It was spectacular. Edgar was a good sport and he loved it, but I loved rubbing my cock against Pierre's in the tight confines of Edgar's ass.

A week later, I was at a lecture at the School of Engineering and Mines, when I noticed the lecturer, Professor Maximilian Schmidt, of the University of Grenoble wore a cock signet ring. I went up to see him after the lecture. He saw my ring and slipped me a note with his address and a time. I nodded. He smiled.

I was at his hotel room at the time he indicated. He was waiting. Professor Schmidt was from Alsace Loraine and very French in spite of his German name.

"I would very much like to spend some time with you. My good friend, John Singer Sargent sent me a note about a handsome Scot he had met. It that you?" he said.

"Yes, I had a most pleasant afternoon with him."

"Alas, I must go to have dinner with a visiting friend." He felt my genitals and smiled. "I would very much like that," he remarked as he felt my cock. I reached over and felt his crotch.

I smiled. "I certainly would like to get better acquainted with you." I said. We understood each other.

"I am going to visit some friends in the country this weekend," the professor said. "You would find them very agreeable."

"I was planning to spend the weekend with friends," I said.

"Let me repeat, you will find my friends most agreeable."

"Well," I said, "My friends are open minded. They are members of the brotherhood."

"Do you think they are liberal enough to find our ways enjoyable?"

"I think they would be very interested."

"Let me know. New men are always agreeable," Professor Schmidt said. "My friends are a cosmopolitan and varied group. Some might even be described as exotic. Does that bother you? I assume you know some men who are not gentlemen?"

"I'm not interested in rank."

The Professor had to leave and I returned to Pierre and Edgar. We went to a performance of the opera that night. It was a fine performance, but it was difficult for the opera to compete with the grandeur of the building itself. The next morning I told them about the professor and his weekend party. I was very direct in explaining the extent of the sexual contact. I was afraid they might think less of me that I participated are these sexual romps. I didn't need to worry. They were both intrigued and willing. Edgar was concerned he was perhaps too old, or had a background that was humble. Edgar had become an officer by merit, not because he was socially prominent.

I told him he needn't have concerns either way. "As far as I can tell interest in and willingness to participate in matters sexual is the sole requirement for membership," I said.

Edgar and Pierre laughed. There was no problem. On Friday, we met Professor Schmidt at the railroad station and took a train toward the Loire Valley. We got out at a small station. A carriage was waiting and we went to an impressive chateau. At first, I thought it was an ancient structure, but I soon realized it was a modern pile.

The Chateau of DeLaval was the seat of the Duc DeLaval. The family's original seat burned during the revolution. The current Duke married an heiress and built the modern Chateau. The heiress was now dead and the Duke made the house into retreat for men of distinctive sexual tastes.

The chateau was a fantasy castle of towers, turrets and pinnacles. We entered into a great hall furnished in the medieval style. There were several men sitting and talking. They were wearing monk like robes. I thought this must have been one of the Duke's affectations, but I noticed some me had the robes open. They were nude. We were taken to our rooms and the butler gave us robes to wear.

I shared a room with Professor Schmidt. Pierre and Edgar were in an adjacent room. Our rooms had a water closet and lavatory, but no bath. That seemed strange to me in this luxurious palace. A man knocked at our door and took us to meet the other guests.

We went through the great hall, and then went into a wonderland. The rear of the house was a great conservatory filled with tropical plants on all sides of a central pool and waterfall. A half-dozen nude men wandered in the room. We removed our robes and entered the conservatory naked.

Professor Schmidt was a surprise to me. In his heavy suit, he was a portly older gentleman. Nude he was well formed and muscular. He shaved his body except for his pubic region

Handsome dark bearded men came up to us. "Welcome to the garden of Paradise. It is always good to see you again, Professor. I am Ali the gardener," he said to those of us he hadn't met yet.

"It is a veritable garden of Eden," Edgar said.

Ali smiled. "We all carry a part of paradise with us," he said. He was circumcised and he stroked his impressive cock. I thought he was well tanned, but he was clearly an Arab or Algerian. A much bigger, very hairy man came up to greet us. He was uncut and introduced himself as Stavros. He was Greek, but had lived in Alexandria. He was a circus strong man and wrestler.

Men seemed to appear out of nowhere to greet us. Several greeted the Professor. He was well known there and seemed to be somewhat of a celebrity, but most wanted to see me, Pierre and Edgar. There must have been at least two dozen men scattered in the tropical vegetation.

We wandered around the room and entered a little area on the side. There was a small Classical temple here. We took a drink from a fountain there. When we stopped, Stavros took his refreshment from my cock.

A gong sounded. That was a sign for refreshments. Trays of fruits, cakes and other delicacies appeared in the central area next to the pool. It was a mixed group of men, racially, socially and physically. In a normal house, one would have expected to be served by liveried footmen. Several men were obviously burly laborers and the Duke himself served a tray. He was an unimpressive man. Naked, he held the tray low so his genitals rested on it. The food had been arrayed in a fan pattern focusing on his uncut member.

The Duke was the center of a group of young, somewhat delicate men. I could not understand what he said, since he spoke French at high speed, but he was apparently funny and he amused the men near him.

The Duke's pre cum drooled on the tray, but that didn't disturb anyone. Edgar was separated from Pierre and me. Ali and several younger, but very masculine men clustered around Pierre.

The conservatory focused on the central pool. We visited the temple on one side. Stavros took us to the other side. The plantings on the edge of the pool were symmetrical, but when you passed through them, this side was more of a gymnasium. It contained actual shower baths and a hot pool. Some athletic equipment sat on the side.

"You like ass play?" Stavros asked us. We nodded. I couldn't tell if he was very direct, or whether his French was so limited he couldn't be subtle.

"You top? Bottom?"

"We like both," Pierre said.

"Me also," Stavros said switching from broken French to broken English. He took us to an area behind the showers where an attendant gave us an enema. Stavros received one too, as did Professor Schmidt. The attendant was most pleasant and he seemed to enjoy his work. We showered and then he lubricated our asses. He gave us a leather pouch filled with lubricating oil.

Schmidt was half-erect as was Stavros. When we returned to the exercise area a handsome man who could have been mistaken for Hercules greeted us. Indeed his beard and hair was done to mimic that of the Farnese Hercules statue. His shaved body was classical, but in place of the statue's fig leaf was a non-classical display of manhood. His equipment could best be described as extravagant rather than classically modest.

"This is Emile," Stavros said. "He is my best friend." They embraced in a frankly sexual way. When they broke apart, Emile greeted us warmly. He had a speech defect, and I suspected he had been born with a cleft palate. This slight imperfection only made the rest of his body and person seem more beautiful.

"Not only is Emile a beautiful man, he is a scientist of the sexual arts. He had the misfortune to be born with a passion for ass sex, but he possessed a small and tight hole." Stavros explained. "Here he explores ways to make the penetration more agreeable."

"I hardly need to say, Emile has succeeded magnificently," Schmidt added. "He did not stop his studies there but he has continued his exploration of ways to make the sexual act more pleasurable."

"The swing is free, M. le Professor," Emile said as he led us though some vegetation to a little clearing. Emile got into a swing or hammock like device. The hammock portion supported his body. It was configured so his arse was spread wide open and easily accessible. His hole was indeed a small pillow of slightly puffy muscle flanked by his massive buns. Schmidt poured some lubricant on his cock and stroked himself to a full erection. The professor possessed a thick organ crowned with a large head.

When his head touched Emile's puckered hole, Emile twitched in excitement. Schmidt pushed the swing away. I realized Schmidt possessed a battering ram, and Emile's ass was the gate to be conquered. Each push of the swing was harder and with each push, Schmidt's cock pushed harder against Emile's hole. I noticed as Schmidt got closer to breaking through, Emile's cock got harder, and he got more excited.

Finally, the hole gave way. Emile was skewered on the professor's organ. Schmidt grabbed the swing and held it tight. It was total penetration. He then let go. Emile swung way, but the return swing impaled him again. This went on for a minute, or more. With each re penetration, Emile's hole relaxed. Eventually the hole stayed open and I could see into Emile's love tunnel.

Unexpectedly this excited me. Professor Schmidt noticed this and he motioned to me. I coated my member in oil and took his place. Emile noticed the change immediately. He tightened his ass as if he were embracing me. I pushed the swing slightly. He was just far enough away so my cock head barely touched his puckered ass. When he slid back onto my cock, it was as if his ass was kissing my member.

His sphincter would gently kiss my knob, and then his ass would greedily gobble up my entire cock. He would try to clamp tightly on my member trying to trap me in his warm ass. Of course, he was too heavily lubricated to hold me. Emile would swing away and we would repeat the sequence again. It was lovely.

It was a very unexpectedly fantasy. Here was a man built like an ancient Greek god. He was big, hard and muscular, yet at his core was a gentle and generous lover. When I said core, I literally meant his core. My cock was deep inside his body and felt nothing but pleasure.

I pulled away and let Pierre enjoy Emile's body. Ali, the Arab man who had greeted us when we entered the conservatory joined Stavros. I went over to them, dropped to my knees and began to minister to their cocks. Both were well-endowed men. Ali was circumcised, and his exposed deep purple knob was bisected with a wide slit. Stavros' foreskin covered his cock even when he was hard. His pink head just barely peaked out of the protective shroud. His cock head seemed tender and delicate.

Stavros collected pre cum in his skin and saved it for me to lick up. Stavros was most enthusiastic. Ali was reserved, but when I returned to sucking him after playing with Stavros, pre cum was always flowing from his slit. Sometime it was only a bead of glistening fluid, other times it was a long filament of cock juices dripping to the conservatory paving.

Ali dropped to the floor and joined me sucking on Stavros' cock. I knew that Muslims were circumcised and wondered if Ali would have a problem with Stavros' uncircumcised organ. He didn't. He also reached behind me and felt my ass. It was lubricated. "I would love to be in you," Ali said. "I would love to shoot my seed into you."

I looked at him and smiled. That was all he needed. Stavros didn't mind at all. He knew Ali and I assumed he knew his tastes. Another Arab man appeared, his name was Abdul and he seemed to be Ali's friend. I later found out he was Ali's nephew. Abdul was young, under twenty-five, I would guess. Had he been a girl, he would have been beautiful. He was tall, slim and elegant with a chest covered in silky black hair and a trail of hair linking his chest to his thick bush. He spoke a little French.

Ali's cock was neither elegant nor delicate. He possessed a battering ram style cock. Indeed, if his cock head had sprouted Ram's horns, it would have been no surprise. Ali looked at me and said, "Abdul, he likes to do you too."

I was a bit taken back by this, but the two men had a plan and I was an essential part of it. Ali and Abdul were lovers, not just fuckers. While Ali was strictly dominant, Abdul was open to all the possibilities. Both were sensual men. While there was continual genital stimulation, there was much kissing and hugging too. Both men must have studied the erotic arts. They moved me into a position that gave me no potential to resist Ali's attack. Fortunately, by the time Ali's knob was at my hole, I had no desire to resist whatsoever. Abdul was sucking on my member as his uncle's cock slid into me. Stavros fed me his member at the same time, so I was fully occupied and happy.

CHAPTER 9

It seems to me that much of the conventional language of sex relates to conquest and surrender. A lover lays siege to his beloved and after a long battle the beloved surrenders and is conquered. The conquered one loses her virginity and is no longer pure. This language is entirely inappropriate for the men at the Chateau of DeLaval. Here all were available and receptive. One needed only to ask and it was granted. The only stress was waiting for the next sexual interlude. For the life of me, I can find no virtue in virginity without pleasure.

Several times a day, hidden servants turned on sprinklers on the glass ceiling and showered the room in warm water. This gentle rain-washed away the semen and other fluids that drooled from the genitals of the assembled men. I was embarrassed when Ali and Abdul's seed drooled from my ass. This bothered no one. Indeed, the Duke himself came up to me, had me bend over and rimmed my ass, collecting the remains of his friends' orgasms. It seems he regarded these remains as a delicacy.

Since Pierre, Edgar and I were new to the group we were much
sought after. Edgar had been afraid he was too old for the group, but
that wasn't the case. He and his genitals were in constant demand.
I didn't know if this was because the group was egalitarian in its
principles, or simply interested in novelty. Whatever it was, the result
was pleasurable.

While I enjoyed many men that afternoon, Abdul, Emile and
Stavros stayed near me and kept an eye on me. We didn't have a
conventional dinner. Food appeared at intervals. This was in bite-
sized pieces called hors d'oeuvres. I wasn't sure I had ever heard of
such things, but they seemed to be the rage here. Meat was served on
skewers. It was quite delicious and exotic.

Professor Schmidt came up to me. "There are two more
days of this; we must retire to the bedrooms and rest. You will be
exhausted otherwise. I was a bit tired and went to bed. He joined me
shortly. I discovered he wasn't entirely sincere about needing rest. His
generously scaled organ had no problem penetrating my ass. One arm
played with the hair on my chest while his cock caressed my rectum.
I was entirely passive. He did all the work. I dosed off several times
to be woken by his orgasms. I had only to enjoy and accept the fruits
of his balls.

I fell asleep with his cock in my ass and woke the next morning
with his cock in place. When I woke, I slipped out of the bed, put on
my robe and went to the pool to bathe. The conservatory was empty
except for servants cleaning and some gardeners. One of these was a
huge man with a shock of white hair and matching bushy beard. He
was directing two healthy lads installing new ornamental plantings on
the edge of the pool. As was the case elsewhere, all were nude.

I went over to him, "The plants are lovely."

"Yes," he replied in a deep bass voice. "The Duke likes to
have everything at its prime." The gardener spoke in refined, educated
French, unlike most of the servants.

"With the artificial rain from the sprinklers, it should ease your task," I said. "Is there an elevated tank to maintain water pressure?" I'm afraid my interests in hydraulics come to the fore even when talking with a naked gardener.

"Several of the turrets and towers of the Chateau hold tanks," he replied. "They look as if they were pure examples of the architect's fancy, but they are most useful for me. I take it you are M. Fairbairn?"

"Yes, I am. How did you know?"

"Emile, the strong man, mentioned you. We are friends, close friends; I am Louis LaFarge, former professor of Botany at the Sorbonne."

When he said he was a friend of Emile, my member began to get firm. My cock betrayed my feelings. Louis was a handsome man, with a barrel chest and strong arms. His hair was white on his head, salt and pepper on his chest and pitch black at his bush. His balls seemed to disappear in the pubic forest, but his cock peaked out. Peaked is the wrong word. It didn't appear to be long, but it was wide. His head was at least the size of an English penny. It was three quarters exposed and his slit was wide.

"Emile said you were a handsome man," Louis said. "Let me show you another part of our water works." We walked onto the temple side of the garden and then under a waterfall. This water was heated and served as a shower bath. He embraced me under the water and we kissed. To the rear of the waterfall, concealed from view, was a grotto room. There was a bed, covered in furs. We got on it, I nursed on his member, and he explored mine. His manhood was massive and hard, but surprisingly tender. I had to stretch my mouth wide to take even the knob, but every movement my tongue made against his cock head caused a reaction. He shivered, twitched and moaned, but most of all he oozed the sweet nectar of his balls.

Louis swallowed my cock whole and worshiped my cock with enthusiasm. I was enthralled as his ball ooze heightened my sexual excitement. He suddenly stopped moving and a second later, he filled my mouth with his seed. He filled my entire mouth cavity, enveloping my tongue in his cream. I was shocked at both the amount and its temperature. It was hot, almost steamy. It was as if his balls were boilers, heating his seed for release. I forced my tongue into the wide slit to stop it up. That dammed the seed in his shaft. I swallowed as he shivered as the fluids backed up. That worked for a few seconds, but then came the flood.

Louis calmed down as the ejaculations diminished. For a brief moment, I was afraid I was going to choke, but once the flow diminished, I wanted to get every drop. His cock head had become acutely sensitive following the orgasm. I continued to lick it. His slit may well have been more than a half-inch wide. I got my tongue deep into his shaft and cleaned up the remaining seed.

While we played, Emile had come into the grotto unnoticed. He slipped his cock into my ass. I hadn't expected that, but it was welcome nonetheless. He pumped my ass as I milked Louis.

"The young man has no need for breakfast, I take it, Louis?"

"None at all."

"I should have warned you, my friend Robert, Louis is an anatomical wonder. Did you take it all?"

I lifted my head away from Louis's crotch long enough to say yes.

"Some men gag, some choke. You are a wonder. Only I have been able to do that," Emile said. He began to pump wildly. He started to moan as he rear loaded me. Louis had a second orgasm, much to my surprise. As man seed spurted into my body, I relaxed and enjoyed the sensations. I left the grotto, showered in the waterfall and returned to the pool.

The pool was empty. I jumped in and swam the length. I heard a splash when I got to the other end. It was Abdul. He jumped into the water and came to me. We talked for a short while. It was difficult, since his grasp of French was limited. Eventually I realized he wanted some private sex lessons. He was new to male sex. He liked everything he had done, but he wanted to learn more, privately rather than in front of two dozen men. Abdul was afraid he would lose face.

The day before I had sucked him and he and fucked me, but I wasn't sure his lips had touched a cock. He told me his ass was virgin. Abdul had no desire to stay a virgin, but he wanted to learn without a large audience. "Your Uncle Ali hasn't deflowered you?" I asked.

He shook his head. "No. I would like that, but he is so big. He is afraid he would hurt me." We got out of the pool and went to my room. Schmidt was still asleep, so I went to Pierre and Edgar's room. Pierre was awake and I explained our problem. I sat down and offered my cock to Abdul. He was uneasy, but once he tasted it, he grew more enthusiastic. Pierre lubricated his cock and very gently opened Abdul's ass.

Pierre's cock was well scaled, but not exceptional. It was ideal for a young man's first foray into anal sex. Pierre took his time and slowly pushed into the Arab's hole. Abdul shook when Pierre's knob popped through the sphincter. Abdul was tense for a few seconds then relaxed. Pierre did what might be described as an anal massage. Abdul loved it. The deeper Pierre pushed his cock, the more enthusiastically Abdul sucked my cock.

Edgar was awake now. Pierre pulled out and let Edgar take his place. Edgar had a much thicker member and it was harder for Abdul to take at first. Edgar was gentle too, and he worked on stretching Abdul's sphincter. I was next in line. Schmidt was up and took my place in the chair. Abdul liked sucking the professor's member. All of Pierre and Edgar's efforts at the young Arab's ass were worth it. My cock slid in deeply without effort. All was well.

That evening I saw Abdul sitting on Ali's cock squirming in pleasure. Both men were in an ecstasy-induced trance. The rest of the weekend turned into a sexual fog. While I met and enjoyed many men, Emile, Stavros, Ali, Abdul and the professor were most attentive. M. LaFarge joined us when he could. Professor Schmidt was right about exhaustion. By the time we left, I needed to sleep for a full day. My vacation was over and I had to return to England.

Life at Oxford seemed very quiet and staid compared to my Paris adventures. That wasn't a bad thing. I enjoyed a quiet life of study. I was interested in my academic pursuits and as I got deeper into my studies, I became more interested and fascinated. Hydraulics was my obsession and I became interested in machinery. My father greatly approved of that.

All work with no play is a well-known problem, but I had a problem with all play and no work. My father regarded his work as being of benefit to society. He felt that if you had a gift for such things, you had to develop it. I was quiet shocked when he told me he was going to remarry. He was nervous when he told me. My father was afraid I wouldn't understand his need for companionship and affection. I understood his needs.

He introduced me to Mme. Willamina Bruckner the next time I was home. Willy, as he called her was a widowed Swiss lady of some accomplishments. She was a painter and illustrator of botanical materials. She began as a conventional lady flower painter, but she had done some illustrations for a learned book for her brother. These were well received and she became a much sought after artist. I looked through one of the books and saw that she combined technical precision with artistic grace. Her illustrations were both informative and beautiful to look at.

When I closed the book, I noted the author's name, M. Louis LeFarge, Sorbonne, Paris. "Is M. LaFarge your bother?" I asked.

"I am his youngest sister," she replied in her French accent. "My parents died when I was eleven. Louis raised my sisters and I. He is a wonderful man. I think I share some of his scientific interests."

Willy naturally was nervous at meeting the grown son of her future husband, but after an hour of conversations, all was well. She was very different from my mother, but they were obviously well suited for each other. Her husband had died in the shipwreck of the

Macedonian five years earlier. She had been able to support herself on her skill as an artist. At first, she had struck me as being a bit plain, but as I have come to know her, I saw she was a handsome woman. I assumed she was in her mid thirties, but I detected no falseness in her affection for my father.

That I was attracted to her bother as my father was attracted to her was a great coincidence. I realized he felt a sexual connection to her. Several years earlier, I might have been shocked to think my father was having sexual relations with another woman. Now I felt relieved. I had worried about him being alone in the great house. They were married in Venice. Willy wanted to see the city. My father returned a happy man. Venice had been a revelation to him. He loved it. Willy embellished the house with sketches of the city. A year later, she gave birth to twin girls. My father was overjoyed. I returned to Oxford.

There was a message waiting for me in my room. It was from Sir Edmund Bannister, the explorer. He was preparing for an expedition to the Pacific to study indigenous plants on isolated islands. His personal secretary had taken ill and he needed an educated gentleman to serve in that capacity. While he knew botany wasn't my specialty, he thought I might like to join him on the expedition.

I was interested and went to see him the next day. It was a great opportunity for me. I sent a telegram to my father asking his advice. Much to my surprise, he was enthusiastic. He and his new wife knew much about Sir Edmund, and my father admired the man. The expedition was to leave in two weeks and that time was filled with activity getting clothes and equipment.

Much to my surprise M. Louis LaFarge, the gardener from the chateau, former professor of Botany from the Sorbonne and my stepmother's brother was joining us. I realized the long boring days at sea wouldn't be that boring. Two weeks later, we boarded the *Cleopatra* for the trip to India and eventually to New South Wales in

Australia. The *Cleopatra* was a freighter that had accommodations for 20 passengers, all members of our expedition.

It didn't take me long to realize not only were the members of the expedition like spirits, the Captain and crew were also members of the brotherhood. Captain Lewis was a handsome bearded man, most distinguished looking. There were two junior officers, Mr. Wyeth and Mr. MacAffee. They were handsome but miss matched. Mr. Wyeth was perhaps 30, thin and rather elegant. MacAffee was fifty, burly and heavily bearded.

Mr. Wyeth seemed to deal with the passengers and Mr. MacAffee with the crew and the boiler room operations. Curiously, I seemed to run into Mr. MacAffee more than Mr. Wyeth did. We had a tour of the ship and the boiler room and my technical interests came to the fore. The boiler fascinated me. Mr. MacAffee was more than willing to talk. I am interested in machinery, but I must admit, the semi nude coal stokers were of interest too. They were not like Greek Gods at all, but they were manly.

We had bad weather shortly after leaving England, and I discovered I wasn't subject to seasickness. It wasn't actually a storm, but what the Captain referred to as high seas. It was very hard on the members of our expedition. Even Sir Edmund, who was nothing if not a seasoned traveler, was affected by it.

One evening during the period of the high seas, Mr. MacAfee and I were the only ones to take dinner. The Captain and Mr. Wyeth were the bridge and everyone else decided to remain in their cabins. We had a long conversation on the boilers and the mechanisms of the ship. The conversation turned to Sir Edmund. He had traveled on this ship several times and I was clear to me that Mr. MacAffee knew of his sexual interests. Mr. MacAfee asked if I shared Sir Edmund's recreational tastes.

"I have to admit I do," I replied. "Does that bother you?"

"Not at all," he replied. "The Captain believes that sort of recreation makes for a happy ship. The *Cleopatra* runs mostly from

England to Australia. It is a long and boring voyage." He leaned near to me. "Frankly it's happiest on the ship when everyone is screwing like rabbits. I don't like love affairs at sea, that causes jealousy, but screwing and sucking just keeps everyone happy."

I smiled. "You appear to be a man of liberal disposition." MacAffee nodded. Dinner was over and he asked me to his cabin. We had just stripped naked when there was a knock on the door. It was a huge man I had seen stoking the boilers a day earlier. He came in and stripped. In the boiler room, he was covered in soot and dust. Now he was scrubbed pink He looked around and saw I was in the room. He looked puzzled.

"It's all right Bull. Mr. Fairbairn is a good man," MacAffee said. Bull dropped to his knees and began to suck him.

"Mr. Fairbairn is a guest," MacAffee said. "Take care of him first." Bull pivoted and swallowed my cock. The man must have been over six feet six, or seven inches tall and was very muscular too. His tongue, however, gently caressed my cock and balls.

"Bull is the strongest back among the stokers," MacAffee said. "They're all strong, but he is the strongest. He works hard every day, but when he gets some time off he likes to play. By the way, he loves man milk."

"I like the cream too," I said. From the way MacAffee talked, I suspected Bull was of limited intelligence.

"I've got lots of cream," Bull said.

MacAffee laughed. "Let me warn you. Bull's balls are full of man seed, but it takes a while to get it out."

"I've got time," I said. Bull stood and I sank to the floor. His cock and balls seemed small in comparison to his body, but that was an optical illusion. I sucked the tip of his foreskin into my mouth then worked my tongue into the pucker to lick up whatever had drooled earlier. Inside the skin, I only encountered the taste of pre cum and a faint taste of soap.

MacAffee stood on the bed so Bull could suck him as I took care of Bull's meat. As soon as MacAffee's cock was in Bull's mouth, Bull's precum began to flow. Bull might be limited intellectually, but he was fully capable of feeling pleasure. This turned out to be a pleasurable experience for all of us.

Bull was a giant of a man, but his sexual equipment was both sensitive and responsive. I did some exploring and discovered the most sensitive spots on his cock. I discovered the filament of skin that connected the foreskin to his cock head was a good spot. It was hard to believe my tongue could lick that spot and drive him crazy.

"Stop it, please," Bull would cry. I would stop and a second or two later he would beg me to do it again. MacAffee shot off and Bull took the load. We took a break to catch our breath. MacAffee dozed off.

"You are a nice man," Bull said. "Do you still want my milk? You don't need to take it. You are fun."

"I would like to take it," I said. "Do you ever shoot it in the arse?"

Bull smiled. His cock had relaxed, but returned to his erect state. "The boys fill my ass," he said. "It's warm and safe in my arse."

"Would you like to shoot into mine?" I asked. Bull looked confused, and then he realized I wanted his to fuck me. He smiled again. He went to a small cabinet next to the bed and removed a bottle of oil. "You fuck me and I fuck you?" he asked.

I took the bottle, coated his cock, and then oiled my ass. I got Bull on the floor and straddled him. His long, slightly curved cock fit my ass perfectly. As his pubic hair touched my ass, I moaned in pleasure. He sat up while I was still impaled and he held me. He held me tight as if he was afraid I would go away. He began to twitch and shiver. I felt his cock twitching in my hole. He was ejaculating. I could feel his sperm tickling my ass lining. It was lovely.

CHAPTER 10

After five days at sea the weather calmed and the seasickness vanished, I soon knew the other members of the expedition. I knew Sir Edmund, Ronnie, his man, and M. Louis LaFarge. LaFarge had an assistant, Wolf Von Babbleburg. He was a Prussian nobleman with an interest in natural history. There were two Americans. Professor Jonathan Whipple was from Harvard and Mr. Jimmy Wilson was from Texas. Wilson looked and talked like a cowboy. He insisted he wasn't. He was a taxidermist. He was a specialist in preserving specimens, both plant and animal. Whipple was a botanist.

Two younger men seemed to be essentially apprentices. They were Virgil Mannington and Sir Lewis Wall. Lord Wall was the patron of the expedition and I soon realized he probably wanted his son Lewis out of the house. I think he hoped an expedition would make a man out of his son. Once I knew Lewis, I realized that was unlikely. Virgil was a studious young man with an almost obsessive interest in botany. He was almost 20, but he looked as if he were 14.

Mr. Sean McHugh was in charge of baggage handlers, the cook and the porters. He was a cheerful Irishman. Because we would be returning with specimens, Sir Edmund wanted porters who could treat them with the care they needed. All of us except for the porters ate in the Captain's dining room. The rest ate in the crew's mess.

We were a congenial group, but I soon became fast friends with Wolf von Babbleburg and with the two Americans. Wolf was perhaps the least Germanic Prussian nobleman you could meet. He was friendly and affable, always willing to help. He was a good companion.

Professor Whipple was an intelligent and pleasant man of wide interests. He was quite reserved until he got to know you, and then was a great companion. By contrast, Jimmy Wilson was the least reserved man I had ever met. He was an excellent judge of character and while he had good common sense, he was imaginative. He was a natural problem solver.

When we got into the Mediterranean, it got warm. Scots either love the heat, or hate it. I definitely loved it, as did the leaders of the expedition. Jonathan wasn't so sure

Wolf was a nudist and spent as much time nude as was possible. The passengers and crew of the ship were all male and no one objected to seeing the handsome and well-equipped nobleman sunning himself naked on the deck. Wolf was a firm believer in the value of sunlight. I'm pale and I'm not sure Jonathan had ever been in the sun. I think he had read about it.

Since we were going to the sunny Pacific Wolf believed we all should become acclimated to the sun. He had been on an earlier expedition and sunburn had been a terrible problem. One man was badly burned and the burn became infected.

Wolf was organized and he had an orderly program of gradual exposure to the sun. It began with ten-minute sessions then went to 15 minutes and then to progressively longer periods of sun. Jonathan was much opposed to this, but Wolf was convincing and Wolf had the support of Sir Edmund. Neither Jonathan nor Jimmy would get completely naked at first, but after a week or so, they relented. We were on the passenger deck, the crew and our porters were on the main deck. Much of the crew tended to go shirtless when not on duty. They rather enjoyed seeing the naked men on the upper deck.

While Jonathan was uneasy taking his clothes off and even more uneasy about being nude, he was a handsome and well-endowed man. One has an image of the lusty and powerful laborer who is equipped like a Clydesdale, and another image of the pale academic with boy parts. God gave Jonathan horse parts. Jonathan was shy and I discovered he was convinced being seen naked would undermine his status as a gentleman and scholar. It was quite the opposite.

I recognized him as a sexually repressed and reserved man. In some ways, I saw in him my own character before in encountered Ralph the Smithy. I wanted to guide him out of this situation. Truthfully speaking everyone wanted to guide him. While this was for his own good, for we all recognized the problems of sexual repression, we all wanted to see what his member looked like fully erect.

It was Captain Lewis and Mr. Wyeth who introduced Jonathan to the world of sexual pleasure. Mr. Wyeth was quite shy, but he bonded with Jonathan easily. From time to time, Wyeth joined us sunning when he wasn't on duty. It would be easy to believe the Captain didn't have any personal needs or urges at all. He was every inch the Captain of the ship.

I knew from Mr. MacAffee that the men on the ship were partial to man sex and that the Captain had full sexual access to them at any time. MacAffee thought this was good. The Captain never abused his privileges and tended to use sex as a reward for good service. "The stokers get to visit the Captain on their birthdays. They love it," he explained.

"They think letting the captain using then for his pleasure is a gift?" I asked.

MacAffee winked at me. "Indeed they do. Although I might add, the Captain is most open-minded when it comes to sex. He likes to please the men too."

"Even the stokers have a chance to take their pleasure of the Captain?" My prejudices came to the fore. I had experienced sex with Bull, the stoker, but it hadn't occurred the Captain had done the same. Even thought I try to rise above class, it seems to rear its ugly head at unexpected times.

We stopped in Marseilles, and then crossed the sea to Algiers to pick up some cargo. This trip was our first exposure to hot temperatures. A month later these temperatures would seem normal, but they were quite a shock to those of us use to Britain's cool and damp climate.

I was sitting nude on the deck with Sir Edmund, Wolf and LaFarge talking when the Captain, Jonathan and Wyeth joined us to enjoy the sun. Many men need clothes to establish their authority. Captain Lewis looked like a Celtic chieftain of antiquity. He was muscular and well built. His hairy body made him look less gentlemanly and more masculine. His genitals were classical in form and unlike the statues, the Captain was permanently semi erect.

Wyeth was tall and wiry with features that are more delicate. He was undeniably handsome and slightly boyish. He was mostly smooth but had a black bush and long cock. I would say he was a little more than semi erect. His big knob peaked out of his fore skin and a bead of precum usually glistened on his slit.

Remarkably, Jonathan eventually seemed at ease being naked. MacAffee later told me the Captain had a knack for getting reticent young man to accept their bodies and be proud of them. "The Captain doesn't have a shy bone in his body. On the bridge, he is all business and you couldn't wish for a better sailor or leader to run the ship. He definitely has a way with men," MacAffee explained. "If you had seen Bull when he came here you would be shocked. Bull was what my mother called simple. He had been abused and mistreated all his life."

"Some men make themselves big men by beating down the men around them. Captain Lewis does the same thing by raising them up. He treats them well and takes care of their welfare. They look on him as a true leader." MacAffee continued. "As far as Bull's concerned, the Captain is a God."

"Every man here has a taste for cock, and most have been beaten up, insulted and abused for it. Here we have our own world where it's safe. Here you can be proud of yourself and find pleasure in men's company. The Captain knows what you want and need. He shares in those needs."

If the Captain helped Jonathan to be at ease with himself, MacAffee did the same with Jimmy. Jimmy, who was from Texas, was a down to earth man much like MacAffee. They got along well and soon got along more than well.

Wyeth was due for his watch on the bridge, so he left. Jimmy joined us stark naked and seemingly unconcerned by his nudity. Jonathan was next to the Captain. He casually leaned over and began to suck the Captain's member. Neither the Captain nor any of us objected in the slightest. A little later Jimmy did the same with Wolf's cock. I joined Sir Edmund and Louis. Louis was equipped with a bottle of oil.

I was on my hands and knees to suck Sir Edmund while LaFarge oiled my arse in preparation for entry. I discovered Sir Edmund's impressive organ and the manly juices that flowed from it excited me. I was apparently most receptive, for Louis' huge organ slipped in deep with almost no discomfort. I was fucked from each end. I was both the receiver of both men's sexual urges, but I was also the conduit of their passions.

As Louis pumped into my hole, Sir Edmund's flow of juices doubled. While the actual sexual stimulation was fine, I also felt affection flowing from their genitals into my body. I had no sense that these two impressive men were using me for their pleasure. I felt we were pooling our resources. I shared my body with them.

Louis began to twitch and shiver. I knew he was filling me with his seed. After his final ejaculation, he pulled out and the Captain took his place. He didn't ask, but he didn't need to ask. He knew. He pushed my legs wider apart so my prostate would be more vulnerable. The Captain's cock was smaller than Louis's and was quite comfortable. He too shot off in my hole.

I didn't expect what happened next. Jonathan took the Captain's place. His huge organ barely fit. It caused an explosion of feeling. It was spectacular. I am afraid I don't know what happened next. The sensations were so intense I lost track of time and my mind seemed to go blank.

I loved it, but I think Jonathan loved it more. He later told me it was the first time he realized the full potential of sexual pleasure. He was shocked when the Captain introduced him to man sex. It had been pleasurable, but still shocking. He led a celibate life and deceived himself into believing it was man's purest and highest calling.

"Truthfully speaking I was celibate more out of fear and cowardice, than from conviction," he explained. "I am cautious and wary of new experiences. It was easier to avoid sex than to deal with it."

"Perhaps you were afraid that you were attracted to men rather than women?" I suggested.

"I'm not sure I could even admit that even to myself," Jonathan said. "To say I grew up totally ignorant of all things sexual rather understates the case. My mother died when I was young delivering her fifth child. I was raised by a nanny who was of the rather strict Methodist persuasion. She was unmarried and was appalled by any reference to sex. My brothers and sisters were difficult and demanding. I was the good child and while my father sincerely loved me, most of his time was spent getting my younger brothers and sisters out of trouble."

"The Captain is a sensual man," I said, "That shocked you?"

"Yes, but in an odd way," Jonathan continued. "I knew nothing of sex, so I had no reason to feel guilt. It was as if the Captain was from a distant land with very different customs. Indeed, he could not have been foreign to me if he had come from Mars or the Moon. It was all new to me."

I told him about my experiences with Ralph in his small cottage. He was surprised that Ralph wasn't a gentleman. I explained that in matters sexual class made little difference. "I don't want to shock you, but I think your huge member would be admired by everyone from the Prince of Wales to the most ordinary laborer. In some ways, sex is the universal language. It needs no translation and is understood by all regardless of class or station." Jonathan understood.

"Did you realize it was possible to feel anything so intense?" he asked. "I had heard the words rapture and ecstasy but had nary a clue as to what they meant."

I smiled. "I was in much the same situation. It was a new world for me. I must admit my vision of life was narrow and monochromatic."

"Monochromatic is the word. It was as if the entire world was black and white and suddenly I discovered color," Jonathan exclaimed. "Everything was suddenly beautiful. One of the reasons I was interested in botany was the color of flowers. When my mother died my family went into mourning and we never came out of it."

"Like Queen Victoria herself?"

"Much like that," Jonathan admitted. "The Captain does not much admire mourning. He feels you must look forward and not live in the past."

"My father is an inventor. He greatly loved my mother but when she died, he eventually moved on. He has remarried."

"I can't imagine my father remarrying."

"He married Professor LaFarge's sister. She is a noted Botanical painter."

"LaFarge is your step uncle?" Jonathan asked. We laughed at the concept of a step-uncle.

"If there is such a thing, he would be that," I said. "Oddly, I met the Professor before I knew of his sister. I found him a most attractive man of great accomplishment. It is odd to think I was sexually attracted to him and my father was attracted to her. They are very different people but they seem to have an allure for Fairbairn men."

Jonathan leaned close to me. "Can I ask you some questions? You seem to be more experienced than I." Of course, I said yes.

"The Captain likes to eat my seed. Do I have to eat his? I'm uncomfortable doing that," he asked. "I like to fuck, but I've never taken a cock in my own arse."

"I wouldn't worry about that. Everyone has his own likes and dislikes," I said. "There are no hard and fast rules on this ship as far as I can tell. I will admit that several things that seemed impossible to me when I first had sex aren't a problem at all now. It takes some time to get use to being fucked, or getting use to sex in general. I was every inch a virgin when I first met my friend Ralph."

"When did he fuck you first?"

"Very soon after we first got together," I said. "I was very excited by him and I confess to being entranced by his cock. This may sound vulgar, but while I like men, I love cocks. They excite me to no end."

"I think I may have the same feelings," Jonathan admitted. "It's hard to admit it though. I hadn't seen an adult man's member until I saw the Captain's organ. I'm afraid I was expecting a boy cock, like my brother's or maybe Apollo's member as you see it in a museum."

"The reality is not very classical Greek," I said, smiling.

"For a second or two I thought it was gross and vulgar. It was so hairy and wrinkly," Jonathan said. He smiled. "That thought only lasted a second. Then I discovered I was excited. When I got excited, the Captain got more than excited. I had no idea a man would be willing to suck on a cock. I had no idea it would feel so good."

"Did you reciprocate?"

"I didn't intend to do that, but I did," he admitted. "It seemed like the most natural thing in the world. You are the first man I have ever fucked," he said. "The Captain asked Sir Edmund which man would be able to take it. Sir Edmund said you were the man for the job." He paused. "It was better than anything I could have conceived. It was lovely."

Jonathan and I talked regularly, and while he was often uneasy, he certainly got accustomed to the sexual world on the *Cleopatra*. He was every inch a middle class gentleman and tended to stay on the passenger deck. With my connection to Mr. MacAffee, I came to know some of the crew. This was due to the birthday celebrations. One of the stevedores, Nigel, had turned 45 and was coming to celebrate with the Captain and Mr. MacAffee. MacAffee was unable to attend and asked me to fill in for him.

"Nigel is a good man but not as bright as Bull," MacAffee explained. "He's a bit thicker than the Captain prefers, so I was hoping you could help him out." I wasn't particularly interested in Nigel, who I didn't know at all, but the Captain was a different story all together. I had no real idea what the Captain was like informally, and I wanted to know more. I arrived at the Captain's quarters after dinner. We talked for a few minutes.

"Mr. MacAffee told you about our tradition of birthday parties?" he asked.

I nodded. "I was told you were generous in your gifts," I said. "I have noticed you run a happy and healthy ship."

"Mr. MacAffee told me you would enjoy this sort of interlude. He said you were comfortable with men of other social ranks."

"I am. It seems to me all men are equal when they are naked and excited," I said. There was a gentle knocking at the door. It was Nigel. He was short, but had exceptionally broad shoulders and a barrel chest. All of the *Cleopatra*'s crew was healthy and well fed. Nigel wore clean clothes and had just had a bath.

"Nigel, this is Mr. Fairbairn. He is a gentleman and a passenger on the ship. He's a good man and wanted to meet you. He likes strong men," The captain said. "Why don't you show him how strong your arms are?"

Nigel flexed his arm. It was almost as big as my leg. I felt his muscles and complimented him. He was rightfully proud of his body and blushed.

"Take your shirt off and show him your chest," the Captain said. Nigel looked a bit uneasy. He was shy. The Captain smiled. "We'll take our shirts off too," he said. Nigel relaxed. "Mr. MacAffee couldn't be here tonight, so Mr. Fairbairn is taking his place."

"He likes to play our games?" Nigel asked.

"I do, especially with a handsome man like you," I said. We had our shirts off now, but the Captain continued to strip until he was naked. As soon as Nigel saw the Captain's cock, he glowed in pleasure. By now, I was naked too. Nigel looked at me and apparently approved of what he saw. He dropped his pants and stepped out of them. He was built with a massive torso on comparatively small legs. Every ounce of his body was muscle with no fat. His chest was dusted with hair and a trail connected it to his thick bush and very hairy ass and legs.

The stateroom was dimly illuminated so I couldn't see his sexual equipment. The Captain was partially erect now and Nigel couldn't keep his eyes off him.

"Congratulations on your birthday, Nigel. You're a good man and a credit to the *Cleopatra*," the Captain said. "Mr. Fairbairn is new here. Would you mind if he were to wake up your privates? I think he'd like that."

"I'd like that too, Captain," Nigel responded. I dropped to my knees and sought out his cock. Only the tip of his foreskin peaked out from his bush. I sucked that into my mouth and I worked my tongue into the pucker. His skin was thick, and it was warm inside. I tasted the remains of soap, and then encountered the some slippery ball juices.

"That's nice," Nigel said. "I'm afraid I might shoot. He's a gentleman."

"Don't worry about that," the Captain said, "Mr. Fairbairn would love to taste the ball juices of a strong man like you." The Captain made that up. He knew little about my sexual tastes. As soon as he said, I realized he was right. I had no problem milking Nigel and indeed, the prospect excited me. As soon as my tongue licked his cock head and caressed his drooling slit, I was excited.

Nigel had a thick skin that eventually was stretched paper thin by his massive cock. It was wide rather than long. I could understand why the Captain might have a problem taking it in his ass. Nigel's balls felt like small apples protected by his hairy ball sack.

The Captain spread a thick quilt on the floor so he could suck Nigel while Nigel sucked me. We traded places a few times. I must admit the Captain's enthusiasm for cock sucking equaled or surpassed mine. Eventually I was on my back with the Captain holding my legs open while Nigel screwed me.

It would be an understatement to say Nigel filled me.

CHAPTER 11

We stopped in Marseilles and picked up some freight, then made the quick trip to Algiers. From Algiers, we were to steam to Alexandria and the Suez Canal. It became very warm as we progressed. I must admit I found this wonderful. I had lived my life in a cold and damp climate. The sun-filled days steaming through the blue Mediterranean seemed almost magic to me.

We were lucky on one respect. Sir Edmund, M. LeFarge and Wolf had no attachment to the English custom of dressing for dinner and maintenance English dress in climates that were entirely inappropriate for woolen tweed suits. The officers wore white shirts and only wore ties at dinner. When they were not on duty, they wore only pants that would have been undergarments in Jolly Old England and no shirts at all. The boiler room crew wore nothing at all except towels to wipe off the sweat.

The *Cleopatra* was a new ship, but the officers and crew were always busy. I hadn't fully realized a steamer's boiler requires constant attention. For all practical purposes, the boiler was a bomb continuously on the verge of exploding. The Engineer and Mr. MacAffee were always alert as were the stokers. He stokers were all men of what we called the lower orders in England, but they knew the dangers they faced. If anything happened, they would all die horribly.

I loved Oxford, but being on the *Cleopatra* made me aware of an aspect of the modern age I had not understood. At Oxford, the dons taught and the students studied if they felt like it. No one was essential for the operation of the University and if a Don decided to take a year off and travel, all was well.

The *Cleopatra* was a sophisticated machine of the most powerful and modern sort. It depended on men to keep it running. Every man played his role and was essential to its smooth operation. It runs for 24 hours a day and for weeks without a break. The officers were either on duty or on call at all times. No officer could decide to rest and miss his watch. The Engineer's cabin was next to the boiler room. He was either cleaning the equipment, fixing it, or worrying about the equipment.

At Oxford if Professor Doodleberry decided not to give his lecture on Roman Literature of the Augustan period, there were no repercussions other than minor inconvenience. If our Captain decided to sleep a day, the *Cleopatra* was endangered. If the Engineer failed in his duty, the ship might well be lost. It seemed to be the concept of upper class and the lower orders made little sense on the ship, and perhaps in much of modern life.

The trip to Algiers was fast, but we had to wait a day to load the cargo. M. LaFarge had connections in the city and he took Wolf and me to visit a friend. We went to a walled house in the Arab part of the city. Knocking on the door an Arab butler let us into a heavily landscaped courtyard. The streets of the Arab section were hot and dusty. The courtyard was what the Garden of Eden must have been like. It was lushly planted and cool.

"M. Le Professor!" a man exclaimed. "It is a great honor the see you again." The man was richly dressed and a nobleman of some sort.

"Sheik Osmin, I am pleased to introduce you to Graff Wolf von Babbleburg, and Mr. Robert Fairbairn of Oxford. They are distinguished scholars and members of our expedition."

The Sheik spoke perfect French and greeted us with multiple expressions of gratitude that such distinguished guests would enter his humble abode. I replied the honor was all ours. We were strangers in a distant land and could hardly have expected to be so courteously received in exquisite home. I assumed correctly that extravagant language was expected. Tea appeared with fruits and pastries.

The house bustled with servants and retainers. Several sons appeared. I think they were sons, but they may have been nephews or other relations. The Sheik was tall, massive and imposing with a distinguished looking grizzled beard and piercing brown eyes. Several older men sat to the side. Several spoke French and the rest sat and looked at us approvingly. Apparently, M. LaFarge was partially responsible for the plant-filled courtyard and the Sheik was greatly impressed with the professor's knowledge of plants.

Two of the younger men spoke English and were interested in Oxford. Murad and Abdul were handsome and in their late teens. They had an English Tutor. Their names struck me as Ottoman, and that was the case. Murad explained the Sheik's father had been the Ottoman ambassador or emissary to Algiers. He had married the daughter of local leader and inherited the title from her family. His grandfather had been a Turk, but his grandmother was Armenian. The family was noted for its tolerance of foreigners and of other religions. "We and our family have prospered greatly," he said.

The house possessed a haman, a Turkish style bath, and the Sheik asked if we would like to use it. He winked at M. LaFarge when he asked. I assume the baths had pleasures other than that of the steam. The house was palatial and straight out of the Arabian Nights. The haman was extravagant.

There was elaborate tile decoration throughout the house, but the hamman was all-marble. It looked more like an emperor's tomb, than a bath. The undressing room was all gold and white; the bath itself was white and green with purple accents. The green was Verde Antique, and the purple was porphyry. This was as close to a Roman bath as I would ever find.

"Normally you keep you intimate parts covered, but the Sheik is a modern man. He and his friends have a taste for younger men," the Professor explained to Wolf and me. "I trust you aren't offended?"

I smiled. "I doubt it would be a problem," I said.

"By the way, you should tell them if you are ready to shoot off. It is polite," LaFarge said. "If you take their seed you will become most popular. This is rare in this culture, but they enjoy it. It is rare, but very exciting for them."

Wolf smiled and said, "I may well become a most popular man."

The haman was hot of course, but the pool was cool. It was fed by a deep well. The combination of Turkish, Arab and Armenian traits made for handsome and masculine men.

There were ten to fifteen men in the bath from time to time. Some were just bathing; others were there for relaxation that is more complete. The Sheik was with five men who I took as his brothers. Actually, two were brothers; one an Uncle and the rest were cousins. Murad and Abdul attended as did several other younger men who spoke only Arabic.

They ranged from being quite hairy to being downright gorilla like. The sheik, a cousin and Murad had thick coats of curly black hair. I assumed that was the Armenian part of their heritage. We were uncut, which was a curiosity for them. The younger men were partially excited, and two were fully erect. That didn't cause any embarrassment. Indeed, it seemed to generate favorable comment from the older men.

Both Wolf and I were soon at half-staff. This caused smiles and approving looks. There was nothing rushed about the time in the hamman. It apparently was a part of everyday life for the men. The Sheik sat next to me.

"Sheik Osmin, your house is magnificent," I said.

"M. Fairbairn, you must call me Osmin. There is no need to be formal in the bath!"

"I am Robert to my friends and I would be great pleased if you would consider me a friend," I replied, and then we talked hydraulics. He was most interested since water was a precious commodity in this desert land. He knew much on the subject.

Clothes make a man they say, but Osmin needed no clothes to be manly. He was an ox of a man, thick and solid. When he was covered in his robes, I would have guessed he was fat. Nude he was a powerful man. His bulky frame was all bone and muscle. In some respects, he reminded me of Ralph, the Smithy, except Osmin was taller and more hairy. His cock was similar, but I guessed it would be larger when erect. He remained soft as he sat next to me. I was still semi erect. He liked that.

"Some English men are so shy, they try to hide their excitement," he said. "I see you are not one of those men, so many of them favor the boys. You are a manly man."

"I find older men attractive. Some say I am of a serious disposition and I tend to seek out mature men," I said.

Osmin reached over and stroked my cock. "I can see you are attracted," he said. "You are attractive too. My grandfather liked taking his guests to the hamman. Of course, there is no way to conceal a weapon in the baths. He had lived in Constantinople for too many years to be unaware of that advantage. It was even more useful here in Algiers. Allah is great, but he had not been able to stamp out treachery."

"I am afraid neither Jesus nor Buddha succeeded in that task either," I said.

Osmin nodded. "In the bath men can neither conceal treachery, nor their passions."

"Was your grandfather a passionate man?"

He nodded again. "He must have been. His wife was Armenian and a Christian, so multiple wives was impossible. She bore him eight children, all sons. I am afraid our seed is potent in the extreme and he didn't want to wear her out. In the haman, he found enjoyment that did not disrupt the domestic harmony. Here it is easy to find men who shared his interests and passions."

"My mother was frail and delicate," I said. "I can appreciate that. Your father shared the same tastes?"

"Yes he did. My mother was the only child of the leader of a great clan. By getting married to my father there was no threat of her becoming a secondary wife. My father treated her with the greatest respect and affection. He became the clan leader when his father in law died. He too knew the value of the haman."

"He liked it both for the protection it provided and the enjoyment it gave?" I asked.

Osmin nodded. I glanced around the steamy room. Wolf was with two older men. He was sucking one as the other sucked him. M. LaFarge was with Murad and an Uncle. They were sharing the professor's huge organ. I reached over and fondled Osmin's cock.

"You are a handsome young man," he said. "And not shy!" He was smiling. I didn't know what was expected in this exotic culture. I had been with Ali and Abdul at the Duke's Chateau, but Osmin was a man of rank.

As I fondled his cock and balls, Osmin whispered, "Often it takes the soft mouth of a young man to wake it up." It was my turn to smile. His sexual equipment was partially concealed in his thick bush, but just his head was a mouthful. He was only semi erect, but I tasted some of his cock juices immediately. All was well.

I assumed he was a top, like Ali the only other Arab man I knew. Osmin was sitting on a marble bench and I was on the floor as I sucked him. My ass hole was exposed. "My Uncle Ali would like to penetrate you," Osmin said. "He is a nice man and most gentle."

"I think I would enjoy your member," I said.

He laughed, "That will come in time!" he said. "I am big. "It is best if my relatives prepare the way. You will enjoy it more." I spread my legs so my hole was more exposed. Ali was a white haired man who was a slightly smaller version of the Sheik. He rubbed some oil into my hole and they slowly eased his cock deep into me. I had not focused on Ali and was pleasantly surprised. When I said he went deep, I understated the case. He was gentle too. It was more of a genital massage than a fucking.

As he went deeper, Osmin got more excited. His cock was monumental, both long and thick. I felt Ali twitching and ejaculating in my ass. When he pulled out another cock immediately replaced him. "Robert, my father-in-law wants you too." Osmin's father in law organ was shorter than Ali's member, but much thicker. He definitely was a fucker, but Ali's load lubricated my insides well.

The flow of juices from Osmin's balls was reaching a flood stage. I glanced up at him. He looked calm, collected and serene. He would have been a good card player. His face betrayed no trace of his state of arousal. The father in law had an extended and vigorous orgasm. With each ejaculation, he rammed me hard. He must have shot a dozen spurts. I felt the seed squirting from his cock like a miniature fire hose. He collapsed on top of me, exhausted.

"My dear Robert, you have inspired my father-in-law. The last time he did this was when he first played with Murad!" Soon I was on my back on a bench with my legs on Osmin's wide shoulders. He cock was fully erect and the cock head was nuzzled in my hole.

"My friends did their jobs well," he said. "Seed is dripping from your ass." He made a quick, hard thrust and he was in. With a second thrust, the curly hairs of his bush tickled my ass. I almost passed out in ecstasy. I became a passive man whose sole purpose was to respond to Osmin's cock and react to his every movement.

Wolf and M. LaFarge later told me I was magnificent. I thought I could do nothing, but react to Osmin's member, but they said I was a full participant. Had I been able to think, I would have recoiled from this subservient role. Wolf told me I had done well. Osmin and his friends saw me as the perfect guest. In a society in which traditions centuries older than Islam were important, the Sheik was a guarantor of fertility and his sexual prowess was of great importance.

The sheik was getting older and had reached the time men's sexual functions often diminish. He demonstrated his manliness with me. Not only had he fucked me to the moon and back, I was a European. There was considerable unhappiness with the creeping colonial expansion of France in North Africa. That I, a European, was the Sheik's sexual plaything was noted with approval.

It was time for us to return to the ship, but Osmin asked if we could stay for the night. This was fine with us. The Sheik dispatched a messenger to the *Cleopatra* to see when the ship would sail. The messenger returned; the ship was to sail at 6:00 the next evening. We stayed as the Sheik's guests.

We had a grand feast that evening. The guests were all male. The women of the household were at a rural home, leaving only the male servants and relatives in the town mansion. The food was good and the men cheerful. That night Professor LaFarge slept with Murad and Abdul. Wolf was with one of the uncles and two nephews.

I spent the night with Osmin and his brother, Hussein. Hussein arrived just after the feast, and could easily have passed as Osmin's twin. He seemed aloof during the feast and his actions were odd. LaFarge came to me and whispered, "Hussein is blind." Hussein was an educated man and spoke English and French well. He was polite and seemed shy.

When we went to bed, Osmin told me Hussein was his favorite brother and a close advisor. "Alas, blindness excludes him from most social life," Osmin explained. "The superstitious believe it is a divine curse and shun him when he is not in my presence."

"He is a handsome man," I said, "almost as handsome as you."

Osmin smiled. "In some ways he is more impressive than me," he whispered. "I think we three might have a good time tonight."

I know you should like a man for what he is rather than for any particular characteristic. Hussein was a nice enough man, but the prospect of his being more impressive than Osmin was exciting. The reality was more exciting than I had suspected.

When we got to the bedchamber, Osmin left and I was alone with Hussein. I disrobed. "Osmin said you are a handsome man," he said. "He tries to find me friends to sport with. It is not necessary. I am content." He stripped off his robe. He was slightly shorter than Osmin and his chest was hairy. I stroked his chest hair. He liked that.

"I am content with my situation. There is no need for you to please me for Osmin's sake," he said. I slipped my hand into his loincloth. There was no need to talk any more. I was odd to be with a man who hadn't seen me. I led him to the bed and removed his loincloth. The second my lips touched his member, he was erect.

Like Osmin, his juices were all ready flowing. Unlike Osmin, he wanted to suck my organ. He licked it a few times. "Once I enjoyed looking at cocks," he said. "Now it is the taste I love," he said. He licked my cock as if it were a rare delicacy. I sucked him as he sucked me, coaxing the sweet fluid from his balls. Hussein was relaxed and unrushed. Osmin rejoined us.

Osmin lubricated my ass and then guided his brother's organ to my hole. Soon I was squirming on it. Osmin fed me his cock and felt a bit like a roast suckling pig on a spit. The night dissolved into a sexual haze. At one point, I was skewered on Osmin's cock and he fucked me to an orgasm as Hussein sucked up my seed.

Later Hussein returned the favor and screwed me so Osmin could eat my sperm. I was afraid Osmin would have little to taste after my spectacular orgasm earlier, but I was wrong. I thought my balls were drained, but Osmin got a mouthful. Later Osmin fucked me as I sucked Hussein. I took his brother's seed. It was more than a mouthful. Osmin told me to save it. He pulled out of my ass, flipped me over and kissed me long and hard. As he did, he sucked Hussein's cum from my mouth.

During the course of the night, the two brothers neither sucked nor fucked each other. I was the conduit for their passion. Apparently, I was the proxy that allowed them to have sex together without violating a taboo against incest.

I also took Osmin's seed and fed it to Hussein. After that, I fucked both of them. I hadn't expected Osmin to open his ass for me. He did it with obvious pleasure. Hussein was to my rear and fucked me again. That is when Osmin got very excited. In Osmin's mind, Hussein was fucking him, not me. I acted as an extension on Hussein's huge cock. I fell asleep early in the morning and woke early unexpectedly refreshed.

We had to get back to the ship, so we dressed and said good-bye. Osmin gave us gifts and letters of introduction to other members of his family in Alexandria and Constantinople. "Show this to any official if you need help," he explained.

Back on the *Cleopatra*, I discussed the night with Wolf and M. LaFarge. Wolf had much the same experience with Murad and Abdul. LaFarge explained that for all practical purposes we were members of Osmin's family now, and members of the clan, he had a similar experience with Osmin's father and uncle years earlier.

"You were found worthy to be the receptor and transmitter of their seed," the Professor said. "Had you been a woman, you would be a wife now. As a male, you are an honored brother. The Osmin's are powerful and wealthy; a letter from them with his seal is of great value, especially in difficult times."

CHAPTER 12

The trip to Alexandria was uneventful; indeed, I needed a rest after my experience with Osmin and Hussein. I did spend some time with the Engineer and Mr. MacAffee working on a problem with the boiler. A valve tended to stick and I found the problem. The two men fully understood the day-to-day operation of the boiler, and I understood the theoretical principles behind the machine. We discovered a curved pipe going to the valve periodically developed a vacuum that sealed the valve closed rather than opening it. A simple change in the radius of the pipe prevented this from happening.

I wrote a letter to the shipbuilding company explaining the problem and the fix. I signed it along with Mr. MacAffee and the Engineer, Harmon. Both men were surprised at this, especially Mr. Harmon. They weren't accustomed to being given credit. Fixing the problem was enjoyable for me, but so too was the time spent in the boiler room.

The boiler room was exceptionally hot and I stripped to only under shorts. The stokers were nude except for a towel. Sweat poured from their muscular bodies. Sweat dripped from their cocks. It looked as if they were continuously drooling sperm, or precum. I found this exciting. Mr. Harmon noticed. "Beautiful aren't they?" he remarked.

"They are," I agreed. "Here we are two thousand years after the great age of classical sculpture, but look at them. They are as well formed as the classical models."

"They aren't very Apollo like to my eyes, but if Hercules is to your taste, they are impressive specimens," Harmon said. I looked at Harmon. He was in his fifties, thin and wiry, but I noticed his pants were tented. He smiled when he saw me looking at his crotch. "As a sailor I've been to Rome and seen the statues. It seems to me our English stokers are the equal to the Greek gods in muscles, but far surpass them when one looks at their privy parts."

I smiled and nodded.

"On most ships the boiler room is a place of horror. It is a death sentence to unhappy men. The Captain runs a happy ship," Harmon explained. "Many men want to command, few know how to lead."

"Your men seem to thrive here."

"Indeed they do. The work is hard, but the food is good and life is not without its pleasures," Harmon said. "Bull much appreciated your kindness. He's never been treated so well by a gentleman of your station."

"I much appreciated Bull."

"He said you were kind and accommodating. There was much discussion among the men. They didn't think a gentleman was strong enough to take Bull's organ," Harmon continued. "They concluded you weren't just a gentleman, but a fine specimen of manliness too. The Captain is like you in that way."

"The pleasure was all mine."

"In that you are wrong. I doubt your pleasure could have equaled Bull's!" Harmon exclaimed. "To tell you the truth, I've never taken Bull. However, I've watched him in action many times. Might I ask you a question?"

I nodded.

"I take it you are a lusty and liberal man. As a sailor, I have had experience with Gentlemen who lust for ordinary sailors. It seems to me there is desire to slum, to have an adventure with a man from the lower orders. I admit many seem to lose their nerve, and only a few seem to enjoy it."

"I would hate to think that was me," I replied. "My family comes from a modest a back ground. My father's eminence comes from his own hard work and genius. I was brought up in a privileged home, but I do not recall a single instance when my parents mentioned class or position negatively. I certainly remember my father speaking of his employees as a fine, hard workers, and solid as a rock, but never as the sort of person who was not of our class."

Continuing, I explained, "I think my interest is in men and the manlier, the more I am interested. It seems that many upper class men are interested in boys, or seek to be boys themselves. That is not my taste. To be completely frank, I like sex with men."

"If perfectly frank is acceptable, my stokers and I share the same interests," Harmon said. "If you were to visit their quarters and the shower room, you and they would enjoy yourselves. It's been a long while since they've had a new cock up their arses, and most have never taken a gentleman's meat. None of them are virgin's but their holes are as tight and firm as a man could wish. As you can guess, they have no problem plugging a willing ass either."

"Am I right in thinking you have no problem either way?"

"That is true. I admit I would love to watch you and Bull going at it," he said. "It would be a treat." We talked for a while longer and he suggested that I come back around five. The passengers normally ate at nine, after the heat of the day. The stokers normally were off from 4:00 to 9:00 in the evening with their dinner at 7:00. I returned to my cabin.

I met Jonathan in the passengers' shower baths. Given the temperatures, this was the easiest way to cool down. He heard about our successful resolution of the sticking valve problem and was impressed. He suffered greatly from the heat. We talked and he asked me what it was like in the boiler room. I began to describe the machinery and the operations of the boiler.

"I'm sorry Robert. I meant to ask what the men were like," Jonathan said. "Sir Edmund told me the men were all but naked."

"He wasn't exactly correct about that." I replied. Jonathan looked disappointed. "As far as I could tell they were completely naked. It is stunningly hot in the boiler room. Nudity seems natural there."

"The Captain told me you have had relations with some of the crew?"

"If by relations you mean sex that I have."

"Was it..." Poor Professor Jonathan Whipple couldn't find the words.

I knew his intent. "It was. It was enjoyable for the crew member and for me."

"I have read Walt Whitman. He honors and reveres the honest workman. I understand that, but it's hard for me to actually conceive of being intimate with men like that," Jonathan explained.

"We all share the same apparatus and equipment and much the same drives," I said. "If Mr. Darwin is right the drive for sexual union predated university education by thousands of years."

"You don't believe education removes the need for sexual activity?"

"I don't believe that one bit," I replied. "Sex is at the core of human existence. Without it, we vanish as a species. Pretending not to care about sex is an affectation, or a perversion. The humblest workman feels the same urges we do. Fate has left him with a different education and a different salary, but I assure you, his cock feels as much as ours do." As we talked, I mentioned I was visiting the stokers later in the day. Jonathan wanted to come with me. At first I told him no.

Sex isn't a spectators sport as far as I'm concerned. I don't think of it as a play and audience situation. I have been in group situations, but while the members of the group may watch sometimes, they are participants in the group activity. Every time I watch men having sex, I seem to join them. I explained this to Jonathan. He understood.

"I would like to go with you and join in," Jonathan said.

"This is not going to be a lecture on a learned subject," I emphasized. "These men like to fuck and be fucked."

"That is fine with me. I can do it."

"Have you been fucked?"

Jonathan nodded. "The Captain did it first. It hurt some, but I was so excited by the Captain, it was fine. Then Mr. Wyeth, Sir Edmund and Jimmy all did it."

"And you want more?"

"This may sound strange, but the more I do it the more want to do it," Jonathan said in a whisper. "Truthfully speaking, I didn't know you could feel as much. When I first played with the Captain, I was horrified he might spill his manly juices on my body, or he might shoot his seed into my mouth. Sucking him was like sucking a loaded gun. Now I could take a bath in cum and brush my teeth every night in man seed."

I told him I would speak to Mr. Harmon and see if another gentleman would be welcome. Jonathan left and I went back to the boiler room. Mr., Harmon had no problem at all. Jonathan and I got to the stokers quarters at five. Mr. Harmon greeted us and introduced us to two of the men, Basil and Gordy. He said we would be taking a shower bath with them.

We stripped and went into the small shower. The room was eight by six feet with two showerheads. Basil was brawny and covered in black hair from head to toe. The coal dust made him look even darker. Gordy was quite small, but just as muscular.

I must admit Jonathan got off to a good start by getting erect as soon as he saw them. Jonathan is well hung and while the two men might have been a little uneasy with new men, they knew what they liked. The erection seemed to clarify the situation for the better.

It was hard to say how Basil and Gordy were equipped. The coal dust and soot seemed to concentrate at the groin and it was a dark and forbidding area. Jonathan helped Gordy clean up and I was with Basil. One nice thing about helping someone shower is you get to discover a man's erotic regions. Basil was a crude looking man, almost gorilla like in his appearance. Cleaning made him look more sanitary, but he certainly didn't look like he would ever pass for a courtier at Marie Antoinette's Versailles. His tits were large, pink and sensitive in the extreme. When I touched them, his cock immediately responded. It was built like him, brawny and solid.

After he was cleaned up, I thought his genitals were all goat balls and foreskin. No cock was viable. When I touched his tits, the cock appeared. The skin was thick, like a heavy pastry on a pie. Soon it was stretched paper thin by his massive tool.

I glanced over at Jonathan. He was washing Gordy's hair as Gordy sucked him. Jonathan had lost his fear of working men. As for Basil, when he was excited he got on his hands and knees and opened his ass. I hunched over him, easing my cock into his ass while still playing with his tits. Basil moaned in satisfaction as my member slipped into his hole.

His ass wasn't tight; it was welcoming. I slipped in easily and my meat was enveloped in his quivering rectum. I know many men think of another man's cock invading the others private parts are unmanly. I felt more like my cock had found a home away from home.

As I fucked Basil, Bull and another stoker joined us. There were now seven men in the small room. There was nowhere to turn without encountering an erect cock. Mr. Harmon poked me with his thin and long member. Jonathan helped Bull clean up, but soon

Bull massive member captivated him. Jonathan bent over to suck it. Jonathan's ass was open and Gordy went to fill the void. Jonathan took this well. Gordy wasn't horse hung, but he was well formed.

This was the first time Jonathan had been in a group of like-minded men. All of us shared his interests and desires. Every cock, every mouth, every ass hole was available for his use and pleasure. There were no romantic trappings, no intellectual posturing, all was simple and direct. Personal sexual pleasure and shared pleasure were the only objectives.

I know for many pleasure is suspect. Pleasure of the flesh is the gateway to sin. Pleasure is regarded as almost evil. We were all fully-grown men. We were not deceived as to the reason we were here. No false promises lured us to this place. We received only what we gave. It was only for an hour of enjoyment, but that was the best hour of the stokers' day and the best hour of our day.

Bull bellowed as he released the rich product of his balls. Jonathan was there with his mouth open catching the sperm as it spurted through the air. As the ejaculations lost their power, he took Bull's cock head into his mouth and sucked the remaining seed from the slit. A little later Basil took Jonathan's cum as Gordy fucked Jonathan to an orgasm.

I was with the fourth stoker, who was called Jumbo. Jumbo was big like his name, but was mute. He wasn't as tall as Bull, but he was just as massive. He was shy and I went to him; he was too timid to make an advance. I think he was virtually deaf too. His eyes struck me as lively and I had the impression he was very much aware of the world around him.

I helped him was and noted scars on his back. Like Rob, he had been badly beaten at some point in his life. Later Mr. Harmon told me that for Jumbo the boiler room was paradise of kindness and respect. He had been vilely abused by his family and by his previous employer. That he was fed every day seemed almost miraculous to him.

After helping him clean up, I fondled his balls and cock. He liked that and his cock responded. I dropped to my knees and sucked his foreskin into my mouth. He loved that. As his cock grew, I realized it was somewhat oddly shaped. He was amply supplied with thick skin. Trapped inside the skin were his pungent ball juices.

The juices were thick and gamy. I knew the men showered several times a day and I knew Mr. MacAffee and Mr. Harmon insisted they peel back the skin and clean the head and the foreskin. If grit got in the space, it could be painful. I realized that Jumbo must have produced a particularly strong brew.

His cock head was small, but the slit was wide. When my tongue explored his slit, I tasted the same pungent juices as they emerged from his balls. He head was quite sensitive in spite of its small size.

Fully erect his cock was shaped like a cucumber. It was tapered at each end and thick in the middle. When he was fully erect, the thick skin provided a soft wrapping for the hard core. It was as if his cock was cushioned. I got up after a while and Jumbo sank to the floor so he could suck me.

I got the impression Jumbo thought I was a delicate porcelain figure that needed to be treated with care. After a short while sucking me, we went to the quarters where we could get more comfortable. We got in the sixty-nine position. He loved this since my cock was the perfect shape for him to swallow completely. Once it was down his throat he swallowed and the contractions felt wonderful for me. I couldn't do the same for him; he was too thick.

I switched positions and sat on his cock. I covered Jumbo's cock in spit and Mr. Harmon's cum lubricated my ass. My sphincter had no problem taking the tapered tip of his member, but the middle was a challenge. Once it was in, it was a wonder. It was comfortable, but very filling. It was so thick I wasn't sure there was room for my prostate.

Jumbo ejaculated when I was fully impaled. It was a single shot of sperm shot with great force. There was at least 30 seconds or a minute between each ejaculation. Each shot added to the sperm lubricant in my ass and made it more comfortable for me.

It was a wonderful experience for me and for Jumbo. After a minute or so, I slipped into a sexual fog. Mr. Harmon and Bull helped me get off Jumbo. Mr. Harmon told me the rich brew of man juices drooled from my ass when Jumbo pulled out. It was lovely he said. Jonathan and I had to get to dinner, but the hour we spent with the stokers was a revelation to Jonathan.

Later that night Mr. MacAffee told me it had been a revelation for the stokers too. They had not had any good experiences with gentlemen before and the thought we were real men as well as gentlemen. They also hadn't realized Jumbo liked to fuck. They had always fucked him. There was no way to talk to him and he was shy and somewhat passive, so they assumed he liked the bottom. Now they knew he liked to top. They were willing, so Jumbo's life took a turn for the better.

Two days later, we reached Alexandria and we had a few days on land. Alexandria was large and bustling. When were landed messenger brought LaFarge and me invitations from Osmin's brother Omar asking us to visit him. He lived in a house on the Nile near Giza and offered to show us the historical sites of the area. Omar ended by saying if there were other men with our liberal and generous dispositions with us, feel free to bring them with us.

The next day we were at Omar's home outside of Cairo on the Nile. LaFarge knew Omar was a well-known horse breeder and he asked Jimmy, our cowboy, to join us. I had not spent much time with Jimmy, but LaFarge knew him well. I think of myself as a perceptive man, but had not noticed LaFarge had befriended Jimmy. They struck me as an unlikely pairing. LaFarge was a distinguished scholar and I wasn't sure Jimmy had read a book.

Omar's home was more of a small palace than a house. It was larger and more expansive than Osmin's house in Algiers. It had extensive walled gardens and pools and consisted of pavilions scattered in these gardens. In this desert region, irrigated gardens were the ultimate expression of wealth and power. As with Osmin, it was clear Omar was an important man, but it wasn't clear to me from whence that power and wealth derived. The family was Ottoman, and originally merchants of Armenian-Turkish ancestry. They seemed to have intermarried with the Arab leader's families.

As far as I could tell, monogamy played a significant role in his rise. Omar's wife was the sole daughter of a Coptic sheik of great importance in Upper Egypt. Omar respected her religion and her. She died delivering her fourth male child. Omar remarried to the only daughter of a noble Muslim family. All of this sounded like the precursor of a King Lear like tragedy. However, both portions of the family lived together harmoniously. The second wife produced only girls. Omar never favored the males or the females in his family. Omar became the leader of both the Coptic and Islamic tribes.

Omar spoke very good French and passable English. One of his grown sons, Suleiman, was at this house. The remainder of his family was in Upper Egypt. When we arrived, we got a tour of the house. The visit to the Pyramids would take place the next day. Jimmy went off to see the stables, LaFarge looked at the plants in the garden and I, true to my father's spirit, went to look at the hydraulics of the pumping system.

I do not believe in fate, but my father, a good Presbyterian, was much attached to predestination. The same establishment the provided the boiler for the *Cleopatra* made the small boiler that ran the irrigation pumps. It too had a valve that stuck. With a wrench and some tools, I corrected that problem in a half hour of work.

It was the best half hour I ever spent. Omar was a precise and detail oriented man, and the sticking valve had greatly offended him. The boiler was expensive and had been his pride and joy. I was regarded as a genius and my protestations to the contrary were regarded as manly modesty. Omar was forward looking and felt increased technical education was necessary if the Islamic world could compete with the Western nations. He took me as confirmation of that opinion.

LaFarge resolved some problems in the gardens. Omar collected exotic plants and LaFarge suggested relocating them so they might thrive. Jimmy's visit to the stable was a great success. He did not share the American trait of assuming he knew all. He did have some small, but useful suggestions that he presented humbly. Omar's grooms took this very well. Humble and knowledgeable is a good combination.

We ate late after the heat of the day and went to Omar's haman to clean off the dust of the day. This bath was more traditional with all the men using towels and with no genital exposure. Jimmy was with the grooms on one side of the room. I was with Omar, Suleiman, LaFarge and Omar's chief butler, Samuel. He was a Copt.

CHAPTER 13

We stayed in the main room of the bath for a while. Omar took us to a second bath room he called the Paradise Pavilion. It was domed, with a skylight open to the sky above and a large tree in the middle. Planted with exotic flowers and plants, there was a ring of fountains on the edge of the space. At first I thought there were garlands hanging from the tree; they actually concealed hammock like swings. It was a lovely room.

Suleiman and his retainers dropped their towels and got on the swings. Then I realized the function. They slipped their legs into silk ropes. These held their legs in the air and opened their asses. A servant oiled their orifices, then came to us and oiled our members. Omar invited LaFarge to use his son.

The butler took each of us to our appointed playmate. I went to a groom named Mustafa. He was a big, hairy man and as soon as my cock touched his hole, he moaned in pleasure. He spoke a little French and apparently Osmin and sent word I had a taste for older, masculine men. Mustafa was a cousin of some sort. He liked younger men and was both responsive and enthusiastic.

Jimmy connected with a thin hairy groom. It was good for all of us. Technically this could have been called an orgy, but it was both relaxed and almost casual. At first, I thought it was Omar being hospitable to his guests, and then I thought it might be related to our rank. It was almost entirely anal and seemed to be a way for us to become acquainted with Omar, his family and friends. We spent the entire time between meeting and dinner in sexual play.

Suleiman and LaFarge got along well. When I said it was casual and relaxing, that applied only to the initial period. As the afternoon progressed, the action became more intense. What had been more of an anal and genital massage became more intense and sexual. As guests, we topped, but the situation evolved. They were all circumcised, and we were all uncut. They regarded this as exotic. Omar watched my cock as I fucked. Mustafa's hole peeled back the foreskin, but was tight enough to pull it over my cock head when I withdrew. This fascinated Omar.

Mustafa was beefy and hairy like the rest of the family; he had a muscular ass that gripped my cock firmly. His own member was thick too. His cock head was fully exposed and drooled manly fluids. I collected some of this and tasted it. This pleased both Omar and Mustafa.

After a while, I took Mustafa's place on the swing. His fat cock was both filling and enjoyable. I have heard that in oriental cultures it is desirable to make noise as you eat. This is considered a mark of appreciation for a meal well cooked. I was moaning as Mustafa plowed me. This was considered polite. They wanted to hear you enjoying it.

Omar took his turn at my ass too. He was as thick as his cousin was, but longer. He was careful when he entered me first, but got wilder as he discovered I could take it. I came close to shooting. He pulled out just before I shot off. I wanted to jerk myself to an orgasm, but he wouldn't let me. "There is a long afternoon to fill," he explained.

The swing was unexpectedly enjoyable. It was low stress and the connection with one's partner was only the cock. Only the sex organs connected, with no other distractions. The swing was adjustable so the ass could be at the perfect height for each man.

I felt like the pendulum in an over sized sexual clock. Mustafa and Omar were the strikes that rang in the hours. Truthfully speaking they rang in the hours, half hours, quarter hours and minutes. There were four swings. All of their occupants were moaning in response to the throbbing cocks. My mechanical interests came to the fore and I wondered if it would be possible to coordinate the men's moans and create a swing powered sex organ.

During a lull, servants brought fruits and pastries as well as cool drinks. The servants were all nude and completely unconcerned about their nudity as they served us. Apparently, naked and erect men enjoying themselves were normal for them. LaFarge and Suleiman were chatting and clearly, their coupling was most successful. LaFarge's impressive organ glistened with the lubricant from Suleiman's ass. Jimmy had a cluster of men surrounding him. They were the grooms from Omar's stables.

We ate and talked and then men began to return to the swings. LaFarge attracted younger men. He was both manly and handsome. He had a fatherly way with them they found attractive. I later found out fathers in that culture tended to be demanding taskmasters. It was easier to develop a friendship with an uncle. Age was regarded as an indication of virtuous living. M. LaFarge's white beard impressed them.

Jimmy's grooms were all thin, wiry men, weather-beaten and use to hard work and hardship. Jimmy was a more muscular version of them and they thought he was handsome. They were vigorous lovers and that was fine with Jimmy. He could give and take.

After the break, I returned to the swing and was with several older men. Anthony and Sergius were from the Coptic side of Omar's family. Sergius had a massive beard and spoke French. From the way he was addressed I guessed he was a priest, or monk. His cock was long and quite thin. I took it easily. Sergius liked to explore my ass, his knob was broad and I could feel him investigating my rectum. I had not been oiled again, but he was a leaker and his own juices lubricated me.

He was slow and deliberate and we talked as he slipped back and forth in my hole. I mentioned the attitude to sex was casual and relaxed here.

"This is not sex!" Sergius said. "It is only sex if it is with a woman. No chance or pregnancy means it's not sex."

"That makes sense to me."

"The only requirement is that you not spill your seed on the ground," he explained. "That would be a waste. Many feel the seed contains a man's strength. It is better to share it with a friend than to waste it. It is best if you give it to a good friend or a relative. It gives him strength." I must have looked disappointed. He quickly added, "Honored guests are always welcome to receive our seed." I squeezed my ass to thank him. Sergius smiled and picked up the pace.

Sergius had low hanging, bull balls. I felt them slapping against my ass he began to pound me. He suddenly stopped and I felt an explosion of warmth in my ass as his steamy sperm filled my ass. He stayed in until the last drop was in me. I squeezed my ass to milk the seed. That was apparently exactly the right thing to do. He was the first to inject his sperm in my ass, but not the last.

When he pulled out a young man came over and licked his cock, and another cleaned my ass of any trace of sperm. This struck me as a lowly job, but the youths did it with obvious gusto. I got out of the swing and Omar winked at me as he got in the contraption. Swirls of hair surrounded his puffy anus. It was well used. A young man oiled my cock and I placed it at the center of the anus and pushed.

His hole opened and peeled my foreskin back, then caressed my cock head. I had heard Jimmy talking about ass lips. Omar had them. His ass kissed and caressed my knob, and then I would slip deep and rub his prostate. His son, Suleiman, got behind me and eased his cock into my ass. Omar and Suleiman never played together but they watched each other. They seemed to have shared the same tastes. They never made a direct sexual connection, but they were always near each other.

My connection with Mustafa and Sergius had been successful and they brought their friends and relations for me to enjoy. Sergius explained that other Europeans who had visited Omar had enjoyed the hamman but had only topped and been sucked. There had been no reciprocity. This they attributed to European customs. LaFarge, Jimmy and I were fully open to the potential for mutual enjoyment. This was exciting for the men.

Sergius whispered, "Omar has never taken to the swings with a visitor before. You are the first outside of the family." I said I was greatly honored by his kindness.

Mustafa was from a minor branch of the family. He was what we would have called a poor relation in England. Mustafa's visit to my rectum had been an honor to him and he was greatly pleased. While in England a sexual connection with someone from the lower orders was shameful, he it was regarded as indicating generosity of spirit.

Mustafa brought son, Ali, over to me. He was handsome and almost beautiful. He spoke only Arabic, but cocks speak a universal language. Ali was smooth except for a thick bush. He sucked me and toyed with my foreskin. He had a long and quite thick cock. I returned to the swings and let him fuck me. This caused an outbreak of celebration. Not only was I the first European he had screwed, I was the first man to open his ass for him. He had come of age as his member popped into my ass.

It may have been the first time his cock felt the warm insides of a man's ass, but Ali had been watching carefully. He was a master cock's man. He wanted every inch of his cock in my ass and he wanted to drain his balls in me. Remarkably, he took his time. He would build up a head of steam and then relax. He would rest with only his cock head on the dark side of my sphincter. I knew if I just tightened my ass muscles, I could have made him shoot. I tightened my sphincter a little and Ali smiled at me. I relaxed and he cooled off. We understood each other.

We were surrounded by Ali's relatives. I guessed there were an uncle or two, some cousins and a brother in addition to Mustafa, his father. They seemed to be interested in seeing how long Ali could fuck me before he shot off. That was fine with me. They also gave him some helpful hints as to what felt good and would be good for me.

Mustafa and his brother alternated feeding me their cocks. They were half-hard but, still drooling precum and the remains of earlier orgasms. Once and a while someone would take Ali's place. The oil was losing its effectiveness and I asked for more. One of Ali's uncles shot his load at my ass and pushed it into my chute with his cock. That was remarkably pleasurable. Two other men were kind enough to add their loads to my ass and Ali pushed it into my ass.

They sat one of Ali's smaller cousins on my cock as I relaxed on the swing. I'm big and was afraid I might hurt him, but that wasn't a problem at all. He shot off almost immediately and Omar was close enough to take the load. Finally, Ali popped in a spectacular orgasm. The room was filled with applause. A bald description of this event makes it sound demeaning, but it had all the feel of a family reunion. They were all friendly and happy, enjoying me as I enjoyed them.

When they were done, Omar picked me up and took me to a divan on the side of the room. Suleiman was waiting there for us. That is when the real fucking started. My ass was well used and very sensitive after my time spent with Mustafa's family. Omar deep cocked me. My love tunnel was ultra sensitive and I could feel every throbbing vein in his organ. He and I were both moaning as his cock worked its magic.

When he got too close to shooting, Omar pulled out and let Suleiman take a turn. We were all excited and had time for another round of orgasms before dinner. Dinner was a great banquet, and the next day we went off to see the Pyramids. When we returned to Omar's house there was a wire asking that we return to the ship. There had been some confusion and the *Cleopatra* had to leave earlier than expected.

We got back in time to allow the ship to leave the next morning. We got to the Suez Canal and a pilot boarded the ship to guide us. This put an end to our normal routine, since we didn't know if he shared our sexual tastes. I was tired and I seem to have slept my way through the canal to the Red Sea. The pilot left and the voyage became hot and boring. We picked up a new crewman, a steward named Raj. He was a tall Indian with a fierce black beard and massive eyebrows sheltered by a turban. Raj looked more like the leader of an army than a steward, but proved to be a find. He spoke English well and had a ribald sense of humor. I came to know him better later in the voyage.

Mr. Harmon, the engineer, got sick with some sort of a lung ailment. The captain moved him to a cabin on the cooler, upper deck and Mr. MacAffee took over his role with me as his assistant. This was hot and dirty work, but I enjoyed it. My status as a useful man greatly increased with both the expedition members and the crew. The crew had a tendency to see the passengers as baggage.

A steam valve blew in the boiler room and burned Gordy, one of the stokers. I was nearby and pulled him to safety and shut down the control valve that fed the broken piece of equipment. I narrowly escaped a bad burn myself. Sir Edmund and M. LaFarge had some medical knowledge and had some medicines that reduced the Gordy's pain. Sir Edmund and LaFarge nursed him back to health.

LaFarge was acquainted with the work of M. Louis Pasteur and had read about new approach to medical treatment that emphasized germ control. This proved to be most successful. Gordy returned to the boiler room a week later in good condition. This event greatly reinforced the crew's attachment to the expedition members.

I was functioning as a member of the crew, but there were some pleasant interludes. I had a chance to get to know the stokers better. Jumbo was deaf, but not unintelligent. He appreciated the time I spent with him, both sexually and as companions. Many times, I could understand what he wanted. Oddly, Bull, who was of limited intelligence, also understood. We had good times together.

Jonathan also joined us in the boiler room from time to time. He was much enamored with the Captain, and Wyeth, but he felt an urge to experience the pure sexual excitement of the Stokers. He was embarrassed at his urges, but nature is a harsh taskmaster and we have little control of that strongest of urges, the need for sex.

In my cabin, we had whispered conversations about his fantasies. We lay on the bed naked and fondled each other as we talked. Jonathan had fucked Gordy, but as yet, no common man's cock had penetrated his ass. I noticed he had been interested in sperm and had intercepted it mid air on his first visit to the boiler room showers.

I asked, "Do you think you could open your ass to Bull or Jumbo's cock?"

"I really don't know," he said. "I think about it often. I think about you. You are so casual and accepting. Everything seems easy to you. I have no problem with Captain Lewis or Mr. Wyeth."

"Those have been good experiences?"

"They were lovely," he whispered. "It was hard to believe such handsome men would do that for me. They actually filled me with their sperm. I could feel it spurting. I don't know what a women feels when a man fills her, but it couldn't have been better than I felt. I knew they felt the same way. I wish it wasn't called fucking. That seems too crude."

"Have you done the same for the Captain?"

"Not quite," Jonathan responded. "One night I just sat in a chair and the captain just sucked me. I shot off and he took the sperm, but he continued to suck. I must have had six orgasms that night. That was beautiful too."

Two nights later, I had Jumbo in my cabin when Jonathan appeared. "Oh, you're busy," he said. I told him to stay. We had a fine dinner earlier complete with wine and Jonathan was mellow and relaxed. Jumbo thought Jonathan was attractive and, of course, was attracted to the scholar's impressive organ. We sat on the bed talking as Jumbo took care of both of us.

Jumbo was gentle and careful. I pointed out to Jonathan that his eyes were active and engaged. He asked if Jumbo liked to be fucked. I said he did, but I told him I had discovered his true interest was in fucking.

"I hate to sound too scientific, but Jumbo possesses a beautifully shaped cock. Not beautiful per se, but most effective," I explained.

"He looks like a bruiser," Jonathan remarked.

"Working as a stoker builds muscles," I said. "He's just a man like you and me. For years he bottomed because that's what his mates thought, he liked the bottom. I discovered his other interest. He takes what comes his way."

"How would he know what you would like to do?"

"I have a little bottle of oil here. If I were to rub some on your hole, he could take it from there," I said. I could almost see Jonathan's mind working things out.

That isn't what happened. Jonathan pulled his legs up on the edge of the bed so I could oil his ass, but Jumbo's tongue was in the hole before I could oil it. Apparently, this was a new experience for Jonathan and he loved it. Fifteen minutes later Jonathan was fully impaled on Jumbo's cock. Jumbo was a lot thicker than the Captain or Wyeth, so his cock was more of a challenge. Fortunately, Jumbo was sensitive. I think he understood both how excited Jonathan was and how uneasy the man felt.

Jonathan was tight and this felt good on Jumbo's cock. Jumbo took his time. Once he was half-way in the rest just slipped into place. I had been watching Jonathan's hole adapt to the invader when the entire organ vanished into the ass. At first, I thought Jonathan passed out, but then I noticed Jonathan was still hard.

Jumbo stayed motionless for a short while, and then he pulled out leaving only the tip of his cock head in Jonathan's ass. Jumbo slowly pushed it in again. I watched Jonathan's hole quiver then open slightly. Jumbo did this several times until it was a single, smooth movement into Jonathan's rectum.

As he thrust deep, precum pumped from Jonathan's cock head. It looked as if Jumbo was pumping Jonathan's manly juices from his balls. It was beautiful to watch. Jumbo slowly picked up the pace of his thrusts until he was feverishly pounding Jonathan's hole. They shot off together.

Jumbo and I licked the sperm from Jonathan's torso. I licked it up. Jumbo kissed it up. It was as if he was trying to savor every single drop of Jonathan's seed. I slipped a finger into his cum filled ass. The entire tunnel was filled with Jumbo's cream. I slipped the finger in deeper and pressed his prostate. This set off a second round of ejaculations. Fortunately, Jumbo was ready and sucked the fresh sperm right from the spigot. We all cooled off and my visitors left.

I was a little afraid this might diminish Jonathan's attachment to the Captain, but this wasn't the case. The captain saw me the next day. "I ran into Jonathan last night after he left your cabin. He sure was glowing," he said. "I fucked him and it was wonderful. His ass was smooth as silk. It was Jumbo seed?" I nodded.

"I didn't know Jumbo topped," the Captain remarked.

"I'm afraid I introduced him to playing the top," I said.

"Was he good?"

"Very good," I said. "He is both skilled and good at it."

CHAPTER 14

As we steamed south in the Red Sea a ship hearing north warned us of problems ahead. Piracy was a problem in the area. It had been under control for several years, but recent unrest in the Sudan seemed to have stirred up the pot. The Captain set a double watch and decided speed was the best way to avoid problems. The pirates were in wooden dhows and had little chance of catching up with a modern ship under full steam.

This put extra stress on the boiler and the stokers. The Captain came to the boiler room, told the men of the problem, and promised extra wages. That went over well. He also recruited some of our expedition members to supplement the watch. Jimmy, Jonathan and Sir Edmund were willing to help.

My official task had been to serve as Sir Edmund's secretary. This was impossible due to my work in the boiler room. Fortunately, Sir Edmund was impressed that I had other skills and Jonathan took over my role as his assistant. Another ship transferred a passenger and some freight to the *Cleopatra*. The passenger was a Turk named Murad, a huge, massive man of somber and fierce appearance. He looked like my vision of a pirate.

Murad was an agent of Osmin and Omar's family and he had been sent to deal with any piratical interludes we might encounter. His freight consisted of two small cannons. Apparently, Omar's business interests were compromised by the pirate attacks and Murad was to deal with that. The Captain and Mr. Wyeth had naval experience, and curiously, Raj, our Indian was most knowledgeable about guns.

The guns were to be used on land, so I had to design a way to convert them to naval guns. I designed a wood frame with springs and an aiming mechanism. Mr. MacAffee led the construction crew aided by Mr. LaFarge. M. LaFarge had some engineering skills and was most helpful.

We built the cannon supports in a day and Murad was most impressed. He had thought we were a group of English dandies. Raj, Sir Edmund and Jimmy also happened to be sharpshooters. Murad liked this too.

Several hours after we completed the gun mounts we saw a burning ship in the distance. We went to its aid, but were too late. It sank and its crew was lost. Several bodies floated in the water. They hadn't drowned; they had been beheaded. The Captain asked us to increase the speed. I had been operating at full speed too. With the boilers to watch and the cannon mounts, I had no more than 4 hours of sleep in several days.

The captain did not approve. Exhaustion caused accidents he said. He sent Mr. MacAfee and Seaman Evan Jones to the boiler room to relieve me. Jones turned out to be a capable and intelligent man. He could watch the gauges and get me if there was a problem. I was told to get to my cabin and sleep. I thought I was too excited to sleep, but that wasn't the case.

Murad was sharing my cabin, but so far, we had never been in the cabin at the same time. I went to take a shower bath and Murad was already showering. He motioned for me to join him. Clean water was in short supply on the ship and sharing the water was encouraged. By the time we were finished, both of us were erect. Returning to the cabin, we had an enjoyable interlude.

You can't tell a book by its cover and Murad was a surprise. Murad, the man with the cannons, was entirely unlike the naked and erect Murad. His English wasn't very good, but he mentioned Osmin and Omar's names and he seem to have had some knowledge of my sexual likes.

Murad had a long cock, thick, but not massive. When we got in the cabin, he hugged me and we kissed. Perhaps a minute later I was impaled on his scimitar shaped cock. He fucked me for the next hour. It was wonderful. He screwed from the front, back and side. No potential way to get in my ass was neglected. He was forceful, demanding and gentle. He was both a man-ramming fucker and a lover. I think he shot off at least four or five times. I did the same, but I was so dazed I lost count.

I woke twelve hours later feeling good and refreshed. Mr. Wyeth was coming off watch when I woke and we met in the shower bath. Again, we were both hard by the time we were done. This time I fucked him to sleep. I was a bit larger than he was use to, but he took it well. His enthusiasm grew with each penetration.

Mr. Wyeth was handsome, quiet and reserved. He finally surrendered to the sexual sensations and allowed himself to fully enjoy the moment. It was lovely. When I finally pulled out of his hole, he was asleep. I showered again, ate and returned to the boiler room.

All was well there. Jones watched the boilers and got along well with the men. He was slim, dark haired man with a beard. We talked and I realized he understood what he was doing. He seemed to like machines. He had just come on duty, so I had another six hours free. I went up to the main deck.

The guns looked quite menacing and formidable. Murad had one eye on the ocean and another on the guns. He looked like a proud father. I head a distant sound of gunfire. Sounds carry well on water. "All hands to their stations," Mr. MacAffee bellowed. The crew appeared, as did most of the expedition members. There was bellowing from the crow's nest men to the bridge and the *Cleopatra* began to turn to the west.

"Mr. Fairbairn, can you get to the boiler room?" the Captain yelled. "Mr. Jones is needed here." It was framed as a question, but it was an order. I went to the boiler. I later found out Mr. Jones had been in the navy and was a gunner.

We were going a great speed, so the noise in the boiler room was terrific. I knew nothing of what was going on above. The *Cleopatra* interrupted a pirate attack on an Indian merchantman. There were three wooden ships attacking the older wooden sailing ship. Apparently, one shot of the cannon changed the situation dramatically, but the sharpshooters were even more effective. The wind was against us. That of course made no difference in a steam-powered ship, but the pirates could not hear the gunshots.

Pirates were falling wounded or dead, but there was no indication of where the bullets came from. Our sharpshooters had no particular interests in showing mercy. The beheaded bodies of the crew of the earlier ship did not inspire pity in Raj, Sir Edmund or Jimmy. The pirates fled with their numbers greatly reduced.

The entire crew of one of the ships was killed, and a second ship was sunk by the guns. Mr. Jones and Murad made a good team. We slowed down and came beside the Indian ship. It was out of Bombay taking silks to Alexandria and Cairo. Captain of the ship, Mr. Medha, had only two rifles at his disposal, although his crew seemed to have a goodly number of knives. The ship belonged to an important Indian trading company and we were assured of a generous reward. This, of course, we did not accept.

Murad had some extra weapons that we gave to Captain Medha. He also gave them the bodies of the dead pirates. Raj suggested they make an educational display of the bodies for the edification of those who might consider a life of piracy.

This suggestion was undertaken with considerable enthusiasm by the knife wielding crew of the Indian ship. The pirates had died quickly due to the excellent aim of our crew. By the time we left, the pirate bodies, and parts of bodies were dangling on the sides of the ship. I suggested they would be smelly by the time they reached Suez. Mr. Medha smiled at me and said he could live with it.

The telegraphed reports of the attack and our victory reached Bombay before we did, and we were more than well received when we got there. We steamed off and the Indian merchantman sailed to Suez, embellished with its gruesome trophies. The next day we encountered the *H.M.S. Princess Louise* on her way to Australia. We stayed near her and the threat from attack vanished.

Some of the officers of the *Princess Louise* visited us to get information that is more detailed on the pirates. In some ways, I think they were surprised at the informality of the *Cleopatra*. The mixture of passengers and crew who jointly manned the ship and the racial and ethnic variety on the ship struck them as odd. I suspected having a Scots student from Oxford running the boiler room would have been more than enough variety for them. An American cowboy, a French professor of Botany, an Indian sharpshooter and a Turk who had access to cannons was a bit much for them.

The two officers interviewed us. They were quite young and not worldly. Murad said he had just happened to find the cannons, and brought them along because he thought they might be useful. I think they were frightened by the huge man and they let that pass. After Murad left, I told them he probably was a representative of wealthy Ottoman merchants and he was sent to protect their goods and put a good scare into the pirates.

Murad had his charms. One of the officers, Lieutenant Randall, looked at him with a combination of awe and fear. I was getting more experienced and I saw the look included some desire. Mr. Randall was a bland, obviously upper class blond man. As I watched him gazing at Murad, Randall looked up and saw I had noticed. He looked frightened as if he had been caught. I smiled. He relaxed. He understood we were in the brotherhood.

Mr. Jones liked the boilers and the boiler room so I was able to spend more time on the deck and with the men of the expedition. Jones had come from a mining village in Wales so he was accustomed to poor working conditions and working men. He got along well with the stokers. He noted my taste for showering with the stokers.

He came to me. "Mr. Fairbairn, you seem to have a close relationship with the men," he said. "Does that compromise your leadership? I see they are a happy group of men, but do they continue to follow your orders after you've been," he paused, "intimate?"

"I've had no problems," I said. "As far as I can tell they think of it as a reward. They know I will go the extra mile for them, and they will so the same for me. I am careful not to have favorites and to treat every man evenhandedly."

Jones leaned close to me and whispered, "Might I join you?" I of course said yes. We talked for a while. Jones had been the plaything of several of the older seamen. He didn't object since his father was violent and the seamen were good to him in many ways. He had always played the bottom role and wanted to try the top. I told him that wasn't a problem. I was comfortable with both roles as were the stokers.

Mr. Jones wasn't the only one who was interested in new experiences. Mr. Randall from the *H.M.S. Princess Louise* rejoined us. The *Princess Louise* was on route to New South Wales. He had been delegated to report on the pirate situation to the Indian government. The Princess wasn't planning to stop in Bombay. Since we were going to the Indian metropolis, we were to take him and save the *Princess* from a long detour.

The Captain had also noticed Mr. Randall's interests. "Mr. Randall wanted to share your stateroom. I told him Murad was already sharing your room."

"I don't think Murad would be a problem," I said. The Captain raised an eyebrow and smiled. Fortunately, Murad seemed to like young Englishmen and the living arrangement was satisfactory. The reason for Randall's move to the *Cleopatra* seemed slim to me. I later found out the real reason for the move wasn't Randall's interest in Murad, but the Royal Navy's interest in our cannon frame.

My little support was easy to make and required so special skills. Murad's cannon was no threat to a warship, but was well suited for the sort of threats presented by the pirates. It was simple and effective. We did some additional test shots of the weapon and I made some further refinements. Randall was the officer in charge of the guns and he was pleased.

He was more pleased by what happened in my room at night. Randall was Wilmont Randall, the fourth son of Lord Wilton. He had been privately educated and sent off to the Navy at a young age. Lord Wilton was known as the Methodist Peer and his son's sexual experience was greatly limited. Randall had no experience with women, but I'm not sure if he realized his virtue was due more to lack of interest than purity of spirit. He was 35 and this was his first time at sea away from England.

Wilmont's skills were organizational and like the First Lord of the Admiralty in the *H.M.S. Pinafore*, he had escaped sea duty. Indeed that opera was one of the reasons he was at sea. The Navy undertook steps to insure all its officers had sea experience. Until this voyage on the *H.M.S. Princess Louise*, Wilmont had lived in London with a widowed Aunt.

As soon as the *Princess Louise* steamed out of sight, we on the *Cleopatra* resumed our more informal dress. I gave Wilmont a tour of the ship and he saw our stokers naked except for a towel around their necks. He was all but transfixed. He later told me he had never seen naked adult men before. Later that night we retired to the stateroom and he discovered I wore very little. While he was unsure about this, he followed suit and discovered the advantage of near nudity in the heat of the tropics.

Once it was dark, we went on the deck and enjoyed the night air. Sir Edmund and M. LaFarge were nude and entirely unconcerned with that. The movement of the ship made some breeze, so eventually the officers and passengers were nude on the upper deck, while the crew was in the lower deck. After a little while, Wilmont adjusted to the nudity. It was a dark moonless night, and I knew some of the men were enjoying more than the breeze.

Wilmont was also surprised Murad and Raj were on the upper deck. Murad came by and talked. His English wasn't very good, but it was adequate for simple conversations. We retired to the stateroom to sleep. The room had a bed and two cots that folded down for the wall. A small lamp burned giving dim illumination. Murad was a massive, hairy man who seemed even more massive naked.

There were three, full gown, naked men in the room and there was no way to avoid having a cock a few inches from your face. Wilmont was excited, but not sure what to do. Wilmont was on the lower cot. I was in the bed and Murad was on the upper cot. The cots were metal but the support was a wide net that allowed ventilation. Murad slept naked and face down. He cock popped through the net and dangled above Wilmont's head. While Wilmont wasn't experienced at all, he knew and invitation when he saw it.

It was dark and the temptation was too great, Wilmont began to suck the Turk's cock. I got on the floor and sucked Wilmont. He was excited. He had a long, thin member crowned with a mushroom style head. Wilmont shot off quickly. He almost choked me with his seed and I had to swallow several times. By the time I drained his balls, he was asleep.

Murad wasn't asleep. As before, he quickly eased his member into my hole and we had a leisurely and pleasant sexual coupling.

Murad was the last man in the world one would guess was a good lover. He came close to looking like one of those central Asian conquerors, like Tamerlane or Genghis Khan. He was aggressive when he approached an orgasm, but he liked to take his time. He had no problem staying hard for an hour or two and fucking the whole time.

When I sucked him, I discovered he drooled precum continuously. He essentially self lubricated himself and my ass. Wilmont woke while we were fucking. I think he would have been shocked had he not been so excited. Murad was relaxed and he let the English Officer take a trip in my ass. I was a bit shocked Wilmont was willing, but he was a natural. He shot off quickly. He tried to pull out, but Murad wouldn't let him.

When Wilmont finished ejaculating, Murad let him withdraw and they immediately replaced him in my just vacated ass. This greatly excited Wilmont.

"Your seed is better than oil," Murad said in his strong accent. Damn if Wilmont didn't shoot again. It was a good night for the three of us.

The next day I spent in the boiler room checking over the machinery to make sure it was in good shape after the three days of high speed steaming. It was a fine piece of machinery and showed no sign of any problems. I was greatly relieved. Jumbo told me Mr. Jones was a good man and a good sport in the shower baths. Mr. Jones had a glow about him. I assumed he had topped and from Jumbo's comment, I assumed he had opened his ass to the stokers.

I am quite sure the stoker would have accepted Mr. Jones even if he hadn't bottomed, but I think it is better if you both give and take. I returned to my cabin and showered. Murad said Wilmont was with the Captain.

Long ocean voyages can be dreary, but this trip seemed to be filled with event. I got on my bed and fell asleep. I was tired and slept for two hours. I got to dine and ate a little. The heat was building and a light meal seemed sensible. That evening the captain rigged up hammocks on the deck so we could sleep in the open air. That was a godsend, since it was much more comfortable than the cabins. After dinner all pretense of being dressed vanished. The heat was such that nude seemed over dressed.

The Captain believed sex was the best sleeping potion and he let it be known the usual requirement that sex be in a cabin was relaxed. He confided in me, that he wasn't very sure that belief was scientifically true, but everyone seemed to feel better. The captain maintained good morale on the ship. Converting an almost unbearably hot night into a chance for sex was good for the crew.

I know there were those at Oxford who such sexual indulgence was for the "lower orders" only. I can definitely state the passengers and officers of the *Cleopatra* enjoyed it as much as the crew. The heat was good training for those of us on the expedition. Sex was a way to deal with it. Civilization and culture are an overlay on our basic natures. Mr. Darwin suggests we all share a common animal ancestor. While many complain about Mr. Darwin's theories, one must be blind not to recognize the kinship. While I would never recommend abandoning civilization, I think there is a steep price to pay for ignores the realities of one's sexual needs.

The Captain asked me to keep an eye on Wilmont. He confided in me that his meeting with Wilmont was by no means for business. "Mr. Randall is no longer a virgin and his arse baptized with man seed," he explained. "He seemed to take it well, but given his background he might feel remorse." He leaned close to me and whispered. "He's a tight one. If he were in the crew I'd have him do some stretching exercised to make sure his whole doesn't close up again."

"Mr. Randall is much attracted to Murad," I said. The captain smiled. The Captain didn't need to worry. It was a moonless night and Wilmont spent it with Murad and M. Lafarge. Murad had a most successful interlude with him. Murad was larger in length and width than the Captain was, and Wilmont had no problem.

LaFarge was huge, but he used Murad's seed as ball bearings to ease his way into the Naval Officer's body. LaFarge was big enough to penetrate to Wilmont's brain, psychologically, not physically of course. With each thrust of the French professor's cock, he erased another portion of his family's very strict and narrow approach to life.

CHAPTER 15

Our arrival in Bombay was unexpectedly triumphal. We Britons are, by our nature, insular and assumed the pirates were a threat to our shipping ignoring their other victims. Their favorite victims were Arab and Indian vessels. A full report of our victory over the pirates had reached Bombay by wire and we were heroes. Captain Medha was a person of some importance and the company he worked for was large.

Bombay was vast and seemed to be packed solid with every species of human being, from the abysmally poor to the unimaginably rich. As the *Cleopatra* was unloaded, Raj invited us to visit some friends of his. Sir Edmund, M. LaFarge, Jimmy, Murad and I were carried there in rickshaw like contraptions with Raj leading the way. We went out of the city to a walled, fortress like house in a park like setting.

The heavy gate opened as we approached. The front portion of the house seemed to be a business establishment. Passing through a second gate, we entered a quite beautiful garden courtyard.

"We must bathe and relax first," Raj said. "We will banquet tonight." He led us to a space that would have done a Roman Emperor credit. The Indian taste for extravagant decoration was very noticeable. The main room of the bath was a pool, with a Turkish style steam area on one side and a mechanical waterfall in the other. All of the attendants were naked and seemed to have a servile desire to please us.

I was uncomfortable about this, but Sir Edmund was unworried. "You have done a great service for the master of this house. This is expected and normal." Shortly thereafter, I realized there was a sexual aspect to their care. This too Sir Edmund regarded as normal.

"Raj knows our tastes. Our hosts would want to please us," he remarked. I knew there was an aspect of ancient Indian religion that included sexual ecstasy as a part of divine worship. I soon found out it was alive and well in his mansion. I hadn't realized it survived.

Raj arranged for us to be tutored in this form of worship. Looking back, I might have expected to be asked if I wanted to participate in these rituals. I laughed at myself. Raj didn't need to ask me; he knew the answer.

Most of the attendants were sexually relaxed, but some were semi erect and a few were most excited. As a group, we were impressive group of men from a sexual viewpoint. Our generous endowments were noted with approval by the attendants.

Each of us was assigned a group of three or four men let by a Guru. The men in my group were graded in size with one man being a dwarf, and the biggest was well over six feet tall. The Guru himself was of average height for an Indian, but his sexual organs were huge. I had a drink that proved to be an emetic. My system cleaned out in a dramatic fashion, this pleased the Guru. I took another drink that seemed to be slightly alcoholic, and later proved to have aphrodisiac properties. Frankly, I don't need an aphrodisiac to get excited.

I with my attendants joined the other men in the large central pool area we then took a bath in a warm pool.

All of the attendants were with us in the pool. Instead of a washcloth, they used their tongues. As they licked me, their cocks came within range of my mouth. I sucked what I could. Everyone was quite excited by now. I like precum and the men's sweet fluids were both enjoyable and stimulating. This was apparently expected and the supervising Guru seemed pleased.

After getting out of the pool, I got on a table and they continued their ministrations. Every inch of my body was explored by their delicate tongues. The dwarf had small arms. He eased his arm into my ass up to his elbow. He cleaned and oiled the interior of my rectum. It was an odd, but stimulating experience. His little fingers massaged my prostate too. Of course, I was fully erect and the cleaning men liked this.

The attendants genitals seemed to be graded in size. As two of the men licked me and I sucked one, the remaining man slipped his cock into my ass. He didn't actually fuck me. The man just slipped it in, made a few easy thrusts and withdrew. That was true until the Guru entered me. His organ was monumental and I moaned as it penetrated deep into by rectum. There was no pain or discomfort. As it slipped in deeper, the more intense the feelings became. It was pure sexual satisfaction.

When the Guru pulled out, an attendant gave him a carved stone in the shape of a large penis. The Guru oiled it and pushed it in my ass. It was cool and smooth. The Guru left me at this point.

Raj came by and smiled. "You are lucky," he said. "You are one of the elect."

"What do you mean?"

"This is a fitting of sorts. They are selecting men for you to enjoy in this evening. You, Murad and LaFarge alone easily took your

Guru's member. You are one of the elect. It is an auspicious sign. Often none of the initiates can take his cock. The gods of pleasure and fertility smile upon you."

"What is the stone for?" I asked.

"You have been ritually cleaned and opened," Raj replied. "The stone keeps you open for the next event. Bend over, let me see it."

I did. When he saw it, he told me mine was rock crystal. I had been selected for the head Gurus' pleasure. "Mine is jade. I am for general use."

"I'm not sure what I am supposed to do?" I whispered.

Raj leaned over me. "All you need to do is feel pleasure," he replied. "They are thinking only of your pleasure. The Guru's are priests of manly pleasure. They believe the flow of man seed feeds the earth. The ultimate pleasure is generated by men, many men, sharing their cocks and their man juices. You might call it an orgy, for them it is a divine frenzy."

"Is that what is planned for tonight?" I asked.

Raj smiled and nodded. "Yes, Sir Edmund volunteered you for the ceremony. He said you would enjoy it. The gurus were worried you might not be responsive enough. You have allayed their fears. They are most pleased. Indeed, they want to call in reinforcements. There is an absolute rule that there be no pain. That all of you can take big ones is a joy for them."

"Do they all get to fuck us?" Jimmy asked.

"If you wish. You can fuck any of them if you wish. It is what you Englishmen call a free for all, "Raj answered.

"I'm a Christian," Jimmy protested.

Raj laughed. "Some things are beyond religion. We are all brothers of the cock. We share the same interest; we feel the same pleasures. Sperm isn't Christian or Hindu. It's the procreative seed of men."

We took another dip in the pool to calm down and cool off. We all had similar experiences. Jimmy and Sir Edmund had found pleasure in the largest men who weren't Gurus. LaFarge, Murad and I had found it with the Gurus. We played in the pool and waited for the banquet.

Raj told us more about the Gurus. "They live in a temple-monastery in a holy grove nearby. There is a spring in the center of the place that never goes dry, so it is a holy place. The priests and the monks are always nude and unadorned. They never wear anything, even jewelry or a tattoo. Unlike your monks, they do not take a vow of chastity, quite the opposite. Four times a day they must have orgasms and feed the earth."

Jimmy, who was down to earth said, "It's nice work if you can get it."

Raj smiled and resumed his tale. "Several times a year they have a festival when they have continuous intercourse for a day. The cult is popular. They allow strangers into the temple on these feast days."

"I would imagine the monks would get exhausted and tired of the continual round of pleasure," Sir Edmund remarked.

"Not at all," Raj protested. Then he smiled. "The monks are all horny bastards. They don't get tired or lose their enthusiasm."

"When is the next festival?" I asked.

"Three days ago," Raj answered. "The next one is on the equinox, three months away. There is one nice aspect to their ceremonies. After the big festival there rest period. They initiate new members at the festival. The new monks do all the orgasms for this period while the older men rest and save. This is considered to be the best time of the year to take their seed."

"That is why we are here. This is a particularly auspicious time to exchange semen." Raj explained. "The Maharajah's and his closest friends will be here."

"Why are we here than?" Jimmy asked.

"Virgins and guests are needed to share the bounty," Raj continued. He laughed. "By the way, you are virgin from a ritual point of view. "You have never shared seed with the Gurus and their votaries before."

"That's a relief," Sir Edmund said. "I would hate to be here under false pretenses."

"Incidentally, during the orgy, the differences in rank and caste do not apply. Only the cock and balls count for the Gurus," Raj said. "Most of the men were well endowed and all shoot prodigious and multiple loads. Don't worry if the seed eventually drips from your hole. That is a good sign."

The attendants re appeared and removed the stone genitals and re oiled our asses. The party was about to start.

A gong rang and a large door to the side opened. Servants carried in trays of food and then the rest of the guests followed. Another group of servants brought drink and a third brought pillows. All the attendants were nude as were the guests that followed. Curiously, the servants vanished only to reappear when more food or drink was needed. They did not play a role in the divine frenzy.

A group of burly men entered the room next. They were muscular and looked a bit like the strong- men in a circus. I could tell they were use to hard work and labor. In the house, the men wore turbans. These men were turban less and their wild and unruly long hair flowed down their backs. The Maharajah and his companions followed. He was some relation to Raj. The Maharajah was an impressive big man. The final group of guests were the Guru's and some monks. As Raj suggested, most were well endowed and several of the Gurus were monumentally endowed.

A small, heavily bearded Guru was the most impressive. He was small in every respect except for his genitals. He couldn't speak a word of English. He was flanked by two massive attendants. They were muscle men with big black beards. The small man must have been the Abbot.

We formed clusters consisting of one of us joined with a working man, a courtier and a Guru. The Maharajah went to Sir Edmund. I later found out the groups were carefully arranged. Jimmy was with the head groom in the Maharajah's stables as well as the best horseman in the Maharajah's court. Murad was with several warriors and a man who I think was the Chief Officer of the Maharajah's bodyguard.

We sat on the pillows, ate, and drank. The drink was mildly alcoholic, but had aphrodisiac properties. I was with the Abbot, his attendants and two other men. One spoke English and was Raj's younger brother, Ravi, and spoke some English. The other man was the named Vanish and was called Avi. He was a big man, very dark skinned and covered in black hair.

He looked oddly familiar. It took me a little while to realize why. He was a dead ringer for Ralph, except for the coloring. Ralph was as light as Avi was dark. The men were like a photographic print and its negative. I stared at him and he stared back. It was almost as if he was trying to place me. He was puzzled.

Ravi's English was good, but limited. He tried to explain what Avi did without the required vocabulary. After a little work, we arrived at Avi's profession. He was a blacksmith. I was stunned. Ravi told Avi I was a scholar.

As this little drama proceeded, we ate, drank and fondled each other's genitals. We were all erect or semi erect. I was the only white man in my group, and my cock with its pink cock head was of great interests. The Guru played with my cock and balls. I began to ooze precum. He collected some on his finger and tasted it. It passed the taste test.

The Guru's cock was almost gross it was so large. He was hairy and hair grew on his shaft almost halfway to the foreskin. His genitals weren't pretty at all; they were pure sex organ. I knew I would be skewered on it before the evening was over and oddly, I knew I would love it.

As the Guru played with my cock, I leaned over and licked Avi's member. The second my tongue touched the organ, I lost control and tried to swallow the beautiful organ whole. Had I been more reasonable, I should have taken the Guru's member. The Guru laughed and clapped his hands when I managed to deep throat the smith's cock. The divine frenzy had begun.

Perhaps because of the drink I was physically relaxed, sexually receptive and responsive. I don't know how it was possible to be sexually excited and physically relaxed, but that was my situation. Avi moved so I could suck him as he sucked me. It was a perfect fit. If I closed my eyes, I was with Ralph again. He had the same hard cock, the same rich brew of manly juices and the same musky smell.

He pulled his legs up do his hole was open. I did the same. Raj's brother came to Avi and eased his member into Avi willing ass. I was below Avi so Ravi's low hanging balls touched my nose. Ravi's member was long and curved when fully erect. I could taste the blacksmith react as Ravi's cock slipped deeper. I felt a finger massaging my hole. A second or two later a blunt headed cock poked at my hole. I shifted my position a little and a thick man probe pushed through my sphincter. I couldn't see who it was. I didn't think it was big enough to be the Guru's monster. I guessed it was one of his assistants.

Raj told me later that typically the Gurus were the second or third cock to penetrate an ass. Their cocks were so large one or two preliminary penetrations were made by these monks to insure the guest was open and willing. The monks were to shoot their seed in the guest's hole so the entire chute was lubricated for the Guru's entry.

Ravi pulled out of Avi's ass when he climaxed. He was still shooting as he withdrew and some of his seed drooled from the ass on my face. This excited me. As he withdrew, another man took his place. This man was a thickly hung Monk. During the few seconds between the two fuckers, I saw Avi's ass quiver in anticipation. I felt the man in my ass jerking violently as he climaxed in my ass. He pulled out and I felt empty. A much larger member took his place. By the time this man's knob was on the dark side of my sphincter, I knew it was the Abbot. Lubricated by the monk's orgasm, the Abbot's cock slid in without effort or pain. The Abbot and the monk began to chant as they rhythmically pumped and thrust their organs into our quivering holes.

The four of us merged to become a single sexual entity. The boundaries between our bodies seem to vanish as the pulsing cocks began to absorb us. I felt incomplete without the Abbot in my ass and Avi's cock in my mouth. Over the next two or three hours all of us merged. Almost every man there fucked me and I had fucked many of him.

I thought this sense of merger was perhaps a romantic fantasy created in my idyllic Oxford days, but I soon understood that it was common to all of us. Jimmy and Murad, our least poetic and least imaginative members were feeling the same way. Oddly the feelings weren't romantic at all, it was pure sex, pure physical passion without the emotional or romantic aspect.

That might seem vulgar or superficial, but the Guru's would have disagreed about that. Sex is the most intense physical experience a man can have and there certainly isn't anything superficial about that.

While the men, monks and Guru's were evenhanded, I became a favorite of the Abbot and the five gurus are who accompanied him. They saw I was particularly responsive to large cocks. They saw how easily I took the Abbot's cock and wanted share my pleasure. They were all had huge members and the cult requited the fucking be painless. That must have been rare, so I was a prime candidate to give them pleasure.

If you had told me I was going too fucked by twenty or thirty heathen Indians I would have run away in terror. In fact, it was pleasurable beyond my wildest imaginings. The Guru's and their votaries had investigated every possible way to give and get pleasure; it was a wondrous experience.

The Abbot shot his load into my ass as Avi flooded my mouth with his seed. The Abbot's ejaculations were forceful in the extreme and I felt his sperm almost tickling my rectum. An attendant picked me up and carried me to another Guru. He sat me on the Guru's cock. This Guru was older and had a thick white beard and a main of unruly hair. The attendant sucked my cock and balls as the Guru slowly pulsed his organ against my prostate.

As the night preceded the sex, it got messy. My ass filled with man seed and when a new man fucked me, cum spurted from my ass and coated the man's organ and pubic hair. When you sucked a cock or rimmed as ass, sperm got on your beards and mustaches. Eventually our sphincters relaxed. When I opened Avi's legs to fuck him, his hole opened and man seed drooled from it. When I eased my cock into the orifice, he tightened his sphincter and again I was transported back to Scotland and Ralph.

Halfway around the world I was with my blacksmith. What had started with Ralph, Avi completed. I was a new man.

ABOUT THE AUTHOR

Bob Archman is a retired man living in the foothills of the Blue Ridge Mountains in Virginia. He is interested in history and travel. In his writings, he likes to explore the lives of ordinary gay men of different classes and backgrounds. He writes about the men he knows. Most are hardworking men with jobs. Some are professional, others are the men who build, or make things. Few go to the gym each day to work on their six packs. They don't go to the clubs a few times a week to dance. They are the men who go to bed early to get an early start on the next day's work. They are ordinary men who happen to be gay, not gay men who have a day job.

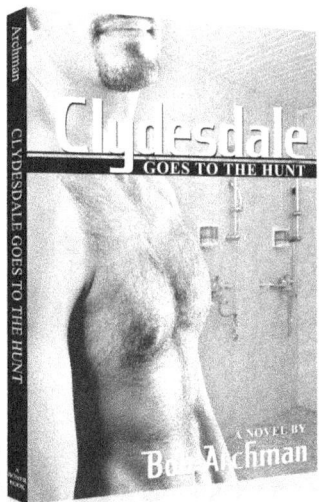

www.ingramcontent.com/pod-product-compliance
Lightning Source LLC
Chambersburg PA
CBHW051125260626
47170CB00005B/1676